KU-485-635

The Princess Splendour

and Other Stories

Retold by Helen Waddell. Edited by
Eileen Colwell. Illustrated by
Anne Knight

PUFFIN BOOKS

Puffin Books: a Division of Penguin Books Ltd
Harmondsworth, Middlesex, England
Penguin Books Inc., 7110 Ambassador Road, Baltimore, Maryland 21207, U.S.A.
Penguin Books Australia Ltd, Ringwood, Victoria, Australia
Penguin Books Canada Ltd, 41 Steelcase Road West, Markham, Ontario, Canada

—

First published by Longmans Young Books Ltd, 1969
Published in Puffin Books 1972
Reprinted 1973, 1974

—

Copyright © Longmans Young Books Ltd, 1969

—

Made and printed in Great Britain
by Hazell Watson & Viney Ltd,
Aylesbury, Bucks
Set in Linotype Granjon

This book is sold subject to the condition
that it shall not, by way of trade or otherwise,
be lent, re-sold, hired out, or otherwise circulated
without the publisher's prior consent in any form of
binding or cover other than that in which it is
published and without a similar condition
including this condition being imposed
on the subsequent purchaser

Contents

Preface

IN 1966 a manuscript which had been lost for thirty years was discovered in a publisher's cupboard. It was the typescript of a number of fairy tales retold by Helen Waddell, the classical scholar, during the First World War.

The history of this manuscript is a strange one. Commissioned by an educational publisher, the stories were considered too difficult for 'elementary school' children. A schoolmaster was employed to simplify them and the bowdlerized versions were published anonymously in a series called *The Fairy Ring*, now long out of print. Not all the stories were used in this way, but the remainder were put aside and forgotten for nearly twenty years.

By 1934 Helen Waddell had made her name as an author and the publishers decided to make a book of the stories they had not used. Later, at Helen Waddell's request, the manuscript was handed over to the author's publishers, Constable's. Once again nothing was done with it until, thirty years later, it was re-discovered and I was asked to select and edit those stories I considered of most appeal to children.

I found that many of the stories came directly from the 'realm of fairy story' Professor Tolkien has described so well: 'All manner of beasts and birds are found there,' he says, 'shoreless seas and stars uncounted; beauty that is an enchantment, and an ever-present peril; both joy and sorrow as sharp as swords.'* Especially was this true of the story of the *Princess Splendour* which has a strangeness and beauty which gives the reader 'a beat and lifting of the heart'. It was difficult to choose between the stories but, by relinquishing some which were more suited for older children and others which had been retold quite recently, I found that I had nine stories which had an unfamiliarity and atmosphere which would, I knew, appeal to children. My second task was to restore Helen Waddell's original text, for the hand of the unknown schoolmaster had reduced the stories to characterless narratives. In the very complicated Oriental tales, it has seemed advisable at times to omit an irrelevant incident for the sake of clarity. Occasionally I have removed an inconsistency which I knew the sharp eyes of children would notice and I have smoothed out the narrative where it was absolutely necessary. I have had always in mind the author's individual way of telling the stories and the pleasure of the children who will read them.

It is an editor's duty to acknowledge the source of story material, but in this collection it has been impossible to add to the scanty notes supplied by the author fifty years ago. *Hasan of El Basra* and *The Magic Horse*

* Tolkien, *Tree and Leaf*, George Allen & Unwin Ltd.

are adapted from Edward Lane's translation (1838) of *The Thousand and One Nights* and the tale of *The Princess Splendour* was published by the Kobunsha in Tokyo in 1889 and came into Helen Waddell's hands in a tattered rice-paper edition, translated by Rothesay Miller. *His Augustness the Prince Fire-Fade* is from the Ko-Ji-Ki, the 'Records of Ancient Matters', and was written from oral tradition by Yasumaro the scribe in the reign of the Empress Gemmio 'on the eighteenth day of the ninth moon of the fourth year of Wa-Do'. Helen Waddell used the literal translation by Professor Chamberlain for her version. The Irish tales, *The Fairy Rath* and *The Crock of Gold* (of which there are many variants) are from Keightley's *Fairy Mythology*; as is also one of the Scottish stories, *The Woman of the Sea*. Of the others, *Gillie Martin the Fox* is taken from *Popular Tales of the West Highlands* by Campbell of Islay, and *The Queen taken by Faerie* comes from the poem 'Orfeo and Heurodis' which appeared in Laing's *Ancient Romantic Poetry of Scotland*. In each case Helen Waddell states that the stories have been 'based on' or 'adapted from' the originals.

Helen Waddell had an international reputation as a classical scholar, her chosen field being the Middle Ages. Her erudition and her facility as a translator from the Latin is seen in her standard works *Medieval Latin Lyrics, The Wandering Scholars* and *The Desert Fathers*. As one reads these books, however, one becomes conscious of other characteristics of this learned woman : her love of stories and her gift for storytelling.

To read *Peter Abelard*, in which she tells the tragic love story of the twelfth-century French scholar, is to realize that Helen Waddell could have made her name as a novelist as well as a scholar, for she could write absorbingly and subtly about people as well as facts. Her love of storytelling is evident too in her delightful books for children, *Beasts and Saints* and *Stories from Holy Writ*.

There were two strong influences in Helen Waddell's life which must have contributed to her love of stories. She was born in Tokyo, her father being a pioneer missionary and distinguished orientalist, so that from her earliest days she was familiar with Eastern stories and poetry – indeed her first book was *Lyrics from the Chinese*. The other influence was her love of Ireland, land of story and song and her parents' native country. It was in Ireland that she was educated, and County Down and her 'ancestral townships of Ouley and Balooley' were always her spiritual home.

Little is known of Helen Waddell as a person for she disliked publicity, but much can be deduced from her books. It is safe to say that she loved children and animals and good company. Again and again we find descriptive details that could only have been observed by someone with a feeling for the countryside and the perceptive eye of a poet. Her sense of humour was delightfully keen. A friend has described her as 'the gentlest of women and one who hated injustice, intolerance, cruelty and war'. The picture that emerges is not that of a dry-as-dust scholar but a woman of warm sympathies, with a deep faith in God.

Preface

In this book, after so long an interval, Helen Waddell shares once more with children her delight in ancient stories.

Loughborough,
September 1968

E.C.

The
Princess Splendour

A Story from
Japan

The Finding of the Princess

TAKETORI lived with his wife in a little house among
the hills of Japan. When a man is old in Japan he hands
over his work to his eldest son, but Taketori and his
wife, O Ba San, had no children. Every morning the old
man went out to cut bamboo and as he climbed the
lower slopes of the forest, he heard the little foxes bark-
ing to each other across the valley. Every evening he

came home with a great bundle of bamboo strapped on his back.

Now it happened one evening that when he was still far from home, he saw a faint light shining in the green shade of the bamboos. There stood a young girl with a light all about her like the shining of the moon. Taketori's kind face crinkled up in amazement, but the girl looked so sad that he took her hand and led her to his home.

'Look, O Ba San,' he said.

'Nara hodo!' exclaimed his wife when she saw the beautiful girl. The smoke-blackened walls of the house were lit up as if by lanterns with the light that was round her. O Ba San petted the frightened girl and Taketori spoke softly to her, but not one word did she say of where she had come from and soon she fell asleep.

The old couple sat and gazed lovingly at her. 'Do you think, husband, that we shall be allowed to keep her as our daughter?' asked O Ba San.

'I found her among the bamboos,' said Taketori. 'We must wait and see if anyone comes seeking her.'

Next day Taketori went to the forest as usual to cut bamboos, but what was his astonishment to find that as he put his axe into the first bamboo, a shower of golden yen fell at his feet. This happened again and again, so that before long old Taketori was the richest man in all Japan.

No one came looking for the beautiful maiden Taketori had found so strangely; he and his wife brought her up as their daughter and, so beautiful was she and so like

14

one of royal blood, that they called her the Princess Splendour. Taketori had a house built for her as magnificent as the Emperor's palace at Kyoto. Round it was a garden with a high bamboo fence, so high that no man could see over it. In the garden were miniature mountains and valleys and forests of firs and a lotus pool. When the Princess walked there in the twilight, it was as though the moon were shining.

So the Princess Splendour grew up to be a woman. 'It is time,' said O Ba San, 'that we thought of giving her in marriage.'

Taketori sat and smoked his pipe. 'I will give her to no man but a great noble,' he said at last.

'And how will you find a great noble to marry her?' asked his wife. 'She is only a woodcutter's daughter!'

'We will give a great feast, wife,' said Taketori. He sent out invitations to all the nobles of that part of Japan, but none of them came to the feast for they were too proud. However, the Samurai, who were their men at arms, came, for they were not too proud to go where the wines were good and the soup of swallows' nests so delicious.

For three days they feasted and at the end of the third day they sat in the dusk with lanterns lit and praised the wine and the host and everything that was his. Then Taketori spoke to the servant who knelt behind his cushion and the lanterns went out and the room fell into darkness.

The Samurai sprang to their feet with their hands on their swords. 'What means this, old man?' they cried.

'That you may better see the rising of the moon,' said Taketori. There was a sound of sliding screens and the Samurai craned their necks, thinking to see the moon rising over the firs in the dim garden without.

Instead they saw the Princess Splendour seated on her white mats with her rich robes about her. The brightness of her presence filled the dark room. For a moment she sat gazing at them and, such was her beauty and gentleness, every man there sighed for love of her. Then she swayed forward in a young girl's reverence to her father's guests and the screens slid softly together again.

For a little while there was silence and then the Samurai cried eagerly, 'Old man, who is she?'

'She is my daughter,' said Taketori quietly. 'Her name is the Princess Splendour.'

The Samurai departed and told their masters of the Princess. Her fame swept through Japan and from near and far men came to see her. They were brought up the stone-flagged avenue of pines and were received courteously by grey-haired Taketori. They were given tea out of Satsuma cups and rare sweetmeats. But the screens that opened to the inner rooms were never pushed back for them to see the Princess. Day after day suitors peered through the bamboo fence hoping for a glimpse of her, but all they ever saw was the gay sleeves of one of her maids. One by one the suitors came to ask her in marriage: first the Samurai, then the nobles and at last the Princes of the Blood. Taketori refused them all.

At last out of those that came he chose five. Three

were the greatest nobles in the land and the other two Imperial Princes. Each tried to settle matters at once with Taketori, but the old man would not answer. 'It is for my daughter to say,' he replied. 'You shall speak to her yourselves.'

One by one he allowed them to pass into the Inner Apartment. They strode in confidently, their silken robes rustling. One by one they came out, their chins sunk on their breasts, for she had refused them all.

At last the old woodcutter went to his daughter. 'Child,' he said, 'this last one you refused was the Prince of Sendai. Above him there is no one in the Empire but the Heavenly Emperor himself,' and Taketori bowed three times at the name.

'If it were the Heavenly Emperor himself,' said the Princess Splendour softly, 'I could not marry him.'

'Why not, child?' asked Taketori.

'Marriage is not for the fairy people,' said the Princess, 'but love is. I love you and my mother but I love no man beside.'

'Daughter,' said Taketori, 'I am seventy years of age and no man lives for ever. When I die, who is there to protect you? Choose one of these so that I may die in peace.'

'Think you they would do some great deed for me?' asked the Princess with a sigh.

'They shall speak for themselves,' said Taketori joyfully and he summoned them all to the Princess. She bowed to their salutations and then she spoke:

'My lords, it is known to you that I am only a wood-

17

cutter's daughter. It is hard for me to believe that such great lords do indeed desire my hand.'

'Let us prove it, Princess!' cried the youngest of the nobles. 'For you I would go through the Even Pass of Yomi!' Now the Even Pass of Yomi is the entrance to the Land of the Dead.

Not to be outdone, all the suitors said the same, for it was a good phrase.

The Princess smiled. 'I shall not send you so far,' she said, and she turned to the Prince of Sendai. 'I have heard that there is in India the Stone Bowl of Buddha. I have ever had a great curiosity to see it . . .'

The Prince of Sendai rose slowly to his feet, for he was a heavy man and slow in his movements. 'We shall drink our marriage-cup in it, O Princess!' he said and bowed and went out.

The Princess turned gravely to the second Prince.

'My Lord Prince of Owari, I have heard that in the Eastern Sea there is a floating mountain, Horaisan, and on it grow strange trees. Golden is their bark and emerald their leaves and their flowers are precious stones . . .'

The Prince of Owari rose to his feet. 'Lady,' he said, 'a branch from that tree shall be the decoration of our marriage-feast,' and so saying, he bowed and went out.

'My Lord Abé,' said the Princess turning to a stately old noble, 'I have heard that in China there are strange creatures called fire-rats whose fur shines like moonlight . . .'

'Lord Abé's wife shall wear a robe of that fur, lady,' said the old noble and he bowed and went out.

The Princess turned to the last two nobles. Lord Lofty's full-moon face was pouting, because he had been left so near to the end.

'Pardon, my lord,' said the Princess gently, 'but this is a hard asking. I have heard that there is a dragon that wears a rainbow jewel round his neck . . .'

'It would better become your neck than his, lady,' said Lord Lofty boldly. 'You shall have it,' and he bowed and went out.

The Princess turned to gaze at the youngest and last noble. He was burning with impatience and her eyes were full of compassion as she looked at him.

'My lord,' she said, 'I have heard that the swallows keep hidden in their nests a little seashell . . .'

The young man flushed. 'O Princess! Is there not a harder task than that?' he asked reproachfully.

'My lord,' said the Princess, 'it may be that you will find it hard enough.' But she smiled at him as she said it and the young man went out lost in dreams.

'Child,' said Taketori, 'there is no shell in any swallow's nest. Fire-rats and dragons and the like there may be, though a man may find his death in seeking them, but in all the swallows' nests I have ever seen, there was never a shell but that of an egg. You have made a fool of the boy.'

'I know it,' said the Princess sadly, 'but I would not have him die.'

The Stone Bowl of Buddha

The Prince of Sendai sat on a silk cushion and drank tea very slowly. Outside he could hear his servants making ready to start at dawn next morning. The Prince sighed, for he was a lazy man and he did not like travelling, even in his litter. The longest journey he had ever made was from his palace in Sendai to do homage to the Emperor in Kyoto, and his bones ached at the memory of it. But India. How far was it to India? The Prince did not know but he feared it must be very far indeed. He clapped his hands and sent for Amma, the blind man who shampooed the Prince's hair and knew all things because he was blind.

'Is it far to India?' asked the Prince. 'Is it farther than from here to Kyoto?'

'Very many times as far, lord,' answered Amma.

The Prince groaned. 'How far?' he asked.

'Eighteen moons for the going and eighteen moons for the returning. Unless one be taken by pirates, or upturned in the water, or eaten by whales, or stricken by sea-sickness.'

'Enough!' said the Prince, and Amma backed out.

The Prince's mind was soon made up. Eighteen moons of travel going and eighteen moons returning: three years altogether! The Princess Splendour was beautiful but she was not worth that. And even after he reached India, where would he find the Bowl? The

Prince sat and thought and after a time his face lit up and he smiled to himself. He had found a way.

The next morning the Prince's litter swung off on its road to the sea with a great crowd of servants following and provisions for a long sea-voyage. The junk was hired, the Prince went on board and the crew pushed off with much cheering. No one knew that the ship only went round the headland to another bay, from where the Prince climbed to his summer house in the mountains and lived there secretly for three years. When the three years were over he went to a little ruined shrine that he had found one day when he was out hunting, and took the old stone bowl that was before the altar. It was dirty and dusty but the Prince did not clean it, for he argued that the older the bowl looked the nearer it would be to the one that Buddha used in India. Besides, the Buddha was poor before he became a god and his Bowl was sure to be shabby. And anyway a woman would know no better.

He put the bowl into a rich silk bag and wrote the Princess Splendour a letter on silk, telling her that he had climbed mountains and crossed seas to find the Bowl for her. All of which was true!

The Princess turned very pale when the bag was brought in. She read the Prince of Sendai's letter and her hands shook. Never, never had she dreamt that the lazy Prince of Sendai would go all the way to India.

'What will the Bowl be like?' asked old Taketori eagerly.

'It will be of stone, clear as crystal,' said the Princess, 'and it will glitter like a diamond in the sun. Open the bag, my father, for I am afraid to undo the knot.'

So old Taketori unfastened the cords and drew out the Prince of Sendai's bowl. The Princess gave one look and gurgled over into laughter. The next morning she sent the bowl back to the Prince of Sendai.

Then for the first time it came into his head to ask old Amma what the Stone Bowl of Buddha might be like. When he heard, the Prince sat and said nothing for a long while. Then he wrote a letter.

The Princess read it in the arbour of the wisteria garden. This it what it said:

Madam and Princess,

The Bowl indeed sparkled when it left me, but its light was put out by the brightness of your eyes.

Sendai.

The Princess Splendour folded up the letter very small and dropped it into the pond and a great carp rose and ate it.

And that was the end of the Prince of Sendai's wooing.

The Jewel-Branch of Horaisan

The Prince of Owari was tall and lean and he sat up late at night and thought too much. 'There is no Floating Mountain in the Eastern Sea,' he said to himself. 'It is a fairytale and the pretty Princess is a child to believe it. But all the better for me.'

So he sent word to the Princess that he was about to set sail for Horaisan, and sure enough he did and no man heard word of him for three long years.

The very day after the Prince of Sendai had written his letter to the Princess, she was walking in her iris garden. It was three years since she had heard of the Prince of Owari and she had hoped that he had given up the quest long ago, but this morning her maids had told her that it was rumoured that the Prince had returned from his travels bringing the most wonderful branch of flowers that ever was seen. Her heart was heavy at the news.

Even as she walked, her maids came running towards her, their gay sleeves swaying. One of them was carrying something and the others fluttered round her like butterflies. As the sunlight fell upon that which they carried, she saw the shining of gold lacquer. Her maids ran to her as she paused on the steps and waited breathless for the opening of the box.

When it was opened, even the Princess cried out for in it lay a branch of strange blossoms, the leaves of emerald and the flowers rose-tinted gems. There was a letter with it which said:

Lady,
   I have plucked the Jewel-Branch of Horaisan. I have still to pluck a flower more precious.

Owari.

The Princess sat very still and her maids fluttered round her in delight. Down the steps came old Taketori, shaking with excitement. The Princess rose and went to meet him.

'Child,' he cried, 'the Prince has come close on the heels of his messenger, weary and wet from the sea. Be ready to receive him.'

'Not yet, my father,' said the Princess, 'not yet.' Taketori was troubled.

'I will put on the robes of ceremony,' said the Princess. 'Bring the Prince to the ante-room and keep him in talk until I am ready.'

The Prince of Owari and Taketori sat in the ante-room and drank the ceremonial tea. The Prince listened with desperate eagerness to the rustling of silk in the room beyond.

'My lord,' said Taketori, 'beguile us with the story of your wanderings.'

There was a sudden silence in the inner room. The Prince began his story.

'It was the tenth day of the sixth moon,' he began slowly, 'that I set sail, not knowing whither I went. Since then three years have passed by and many winds have blown, few of them fair. I have sailed to the rim of the world and looked over the steep edge of the sea. I have lain in dead calm among rocks in the midst of the ocean with my tongue black for want of water. I have seen the heavens open like a waterfall, and the lightning like stairs across it. Once a dragon climbed on the ship and we killed it with our spears. Always we drifted before the wind, for we knew not whither to go.

'But on the seventh day of the seventh moon of the second year of our wandering, I saw far off a mountain peak shining like an iceberg. All that day it floated nearer us but at last we could sail no closer for around the mountain to a distance of half a league the water lay like molten glass and no breeze ruffled it. On the early morning of the next day, I lowered myself into the water and swam to the mountain verge and so did enter Paradise.'

'Nara hodo!' said old Taketori, and his eyes were round.

'The cliffs were steep but I swam to where they opened with a valley between. It was a valley of peach trees in blossom. A stream came down to it and the water sparkled like diamonds. Higher up there was a cobweb bridge of rainbows and over it came a woman, the loveliest in all the world – save one.'

Someone behind the screen caught her breath. The Prince heard it and went on confidently.

' "Lady," I cried to her, "what call you this place?" and she answered, "Horaisan!" and –'

The Prince's voice died away. He rose slowly to his feet, staring at a little procession coming up the garden. There were five men, one behind the other, each clad in blue with the badge of a worker in gold on his sleeve. The leader carried a letter in a split stick. The men came to the steps and bowed themselves to the ground.

'May it please your Excellency,' the leader began, addressing Taketori, 'it is a matter of a small account ...'

With one bound the Prince of Owari was down the steps and clutching him by the throat. The rest scuttled sideways like terrified crabs. The screen in the next room slid back.

'Patience, my lord Prince!' said the voice of the Princess. 'It is perhaps with me that these good men have their affair.'

The Prince's grip relaxed. He turned and went up

the steps to the ante-room and sat there motionless, gazing straight before him. The man with the letter in the cleft stick edged along till he came to the opening in the screen where stood the Princess.

'Is it for this you would be paid?' asked the Princess, pointing to the Jewel-Branch that lay at her feet.

'The very same, my lady.'

'It was you who made it?'

'It was, my lady. Three years' work is in it, day and night.'

'And who gave you the task?'

'My lord Prince, my lady. For your marriage gift it was and he looked to every leaf of it himself. I hope it is to your liking, my lady. It was to be a great surprise for your ladyship.'

'And so indeed it was,' said the Princess smiling. 'And now you have come for payment?'

'We be poor men, my lady. My lord Prince – it was not convenient for him to pay at the time – there was a saying that he was marrying today ...'

There was a chiming of gold pieces and one of the Princess's maids came out carrying the lacquer box heaped with golden yen. 'Is it enough?' asked the Princess.

'May the stork and the tortoise ...' began the leader delightedly, chanting the marriage blessing.

'Enough!' said the Princess and the procession departed, bowing at every step, while the Princess passed silently into her apartments again.

The Prince of Owari sat motionless as Taketori

gently laid the Jewel-Branch before him. In a little while the Princess heard the verandah creak under his departing footsteps.

And that was the end of the Prince of Owari's wooing.

The Robe of Fire-Rats' Fur

It was the time of the Great Cold and the snow was deep. In the Inner Apartment the shutters were drawn close and the Princess and her maids were gathered round the fire where the charcoal glowed in its bed of white ash. 'I wish,' said the Princess laughing, 'that my Lord Abé would bring me the robe of fire-rats' fur.'

The screens slid back and old Taketori appeared. 'Child,' he said, 'the third of the suitors is here. My Lord Abé awaits without and bids me say that he presents you with this, on his knees.'

The Princess rose, trembling. The lid of the box was thick with jewels and beneath it lay a shimmering robe of frosted fur. She slipped it over her shoulders and her maids exclaimed with delight. 'Moonlight on snow!' they cried. Then her father took the Princess by the hand and led her into the ante-room.

The old lord bowed his fine grey head to the floor. 'Lady,' he said, 'almost is it reward enough to see you wear my robe.'

'My lord,' said the Princess, speaking very low, 'was it hard to win?'

'I am too old to adventure as did the Princes of Sendai

and Owari,' said the Lord Abé, 'but I have wealth and good friends and I used them. There was but one such robe, they told me, in all China and that was in the monastery of the Lianshan mountains. Now it is no longer in the monastery, Lady.'

'My lord,' said the Princess, 'I fear you have beggared yourself.'

'Lady,' said Lord Abé, 'I have seen you wear it.' He bowed again to her and so dignified and stately was he that the Princess's heart was soft towards him, for all her dread that he had been successful.

'Lady,' said the old lord gravely, 'I have heard that my rivals sought to win you by a trick. Is there a test by which you may prove me?'

The Princess hesitated. 'I have heard,' she said slowly, 'that the skin of a fire-rat does not burn if passed through fire.'

'So have I also heard,' said Lord Abé. He slipped the robe from the shoulders of the Princess and laid it on the fire. There was a sharp hissing and a smell of scorching fur. The Princess sprang forward to save the robe, but Lord Abé bade her stay. 'Small matter,' he said, 'since I have lost a greater thing.'

As the fire ran through the robe, he took the tongs and thrust it deeper into the glowing charcoal.

'My lord,' said the Princess through her tears, 'you have proved your faith.'

The old lord bowed again. 'Lady,' he said, 'you are very gracious. Did I not say that it was reward enough to see you wear my robe?'

And he took his leave, for this was the end of the Lord Abé's wooing.

The Dragon Jewel

Lord Lofty sat on the dais and his silken robes spread stiffly round him as he looked on the faces of his Samurai, ranked in the hall below him.

'You have heard of the rainbow jewel on the Dragon's neck,' he asked. 'It is my will that you find it.'

The Samurai stirred uneasily and looked at one another. 'My lord,' said the oldest of them, 'it is for dragons to fight with dragons and we are men.'

Lord Lofty held out his arm and his long sleeve swept the mats. 'Which of you brings me the Dragon Jewel,' he said, 'shall have his sleeves filled with golden yen. And if he be killed by the Dragon, I will myself offer a bowl of rice to his spirit when I worship in the Temple of my Ancestors.'

The oldest of the Samurai answered again. 'My lord, I have heard that there is a tortoise which has been dead these three thousand years. His Highness the Prince of Chu keeps it in a lacquer box on the altar of the shrine of his August Ancestors. My lord, would that tortoise rather be dead and its person worshipped among the August Ancestors, or be alive and wagging its tail in the mud?'

'Wagging its tail in the mud, I suppose,' said Lord Lofty sulkily.

'So choose we all,' said the Samurai.

Then Lord Lofty became very angry. He stormed at them and ordered them not to see his face again until they brought the Dragon Jewel with them. He gave them much money for the journey and they went away and spent it, nor had they any desire to come back.

For a year Lord Lofty was well content. He built a grand palace for the Princess Splendour, while he waited for the Samurai to return. But when the last verandah was polished and the last scroll hung, his impatience became so great that he resolved to set out himself to find the dragon.

He stood on the deck of his junk and shook his bow and arrows at the sea and sky and challenged all dragons to fight him. So they sailed into the West and Lord Lofty was very sea-sick, but he saw no dragons.

On the third day came the typhoon and the junk ran before it. The heavens were black and the Thunder God beat his drums, the rain fell like rods and the sea rose to meet the sky. The pilot lifted his voice and wept and said the wrath of the gods was above them, and the wrath of the dragons below them, and it was all Lord Lofty's fault. Then Lord Lofty's heart died within him and he fell on his knees and prayed to all dragons to pardon him, for he was a vain and foolish man. As he prayed the roll of the drums grew faint, the waves swung less furiously and the wind blew them to the country of Harima in the Inland Sea where they cast anchor at dawn. But Lord Lofty lay in the bottom of the boat and there was no spirit left in him.

They lifted him out on a mat and laid him under a tree to dry. The Governor of Harima sent him home in his own litter. The peasants along the road rushed out asking to see the jewel from the Dragon's neck, but Lord Lofty thrust his head through the curtains of the litter and bellowed at them.

When the Samurai heard that their lord had come home in such a grievous state, they confessed all that they had done. Lord Lofty looked at them and smiled ruefully.

'You are wise men,' he said. 'Live and wag your tails in the mud and I will join you. What little I have left, you shall share, for I have had enough of women.'

And that was the end of Lord Lofty's wooing.

The Shell in the Swallows' Nest

The youngest of the nobles had far to go. His home was among the mountains of the South and at the end of the first day's journey he lodged for the night in a little village inn at the foot of the Great Pass. He sat on the worn yellow mats in the best room and the old man who was the host of the inn served him with brown arrow-root and asked pardon for the smoke and the unworthiness of everything that was his.

The youngest of the nobles smiled at him, but his eyes were on the darting swallows as they dipped in and out under the eaves. His heart was very sore. Was it a boy she thought him that she had set him to robbing swallows' nests?

'Old man,' he said abruptly, 'have you ever heard that the swallows keep a sea-shell hidden in their nests?'

The old man shook his head. 'Many a swallows' nest have I seen, but never any holding but the shell of an egg. But the old man my father...'

'Bring him to me,' said the youngest of the nobles and the inn-keeper bowed himself out.

O Ji San had a wise, wrinkled face and a high quavering voice. He remembered well hearing the saying 'As hard to find as the shell in a swallow's nest'. Many a time as a boy he had climbed to the thatch of the kitchen of the great lord's house on the hill where the swallows built their nests. He had heard say that you could find the shell if you caught the swallow just before it laid its egg. Seven times the swallows turn round and flirt their tails before they lay their eggs and if you slipped your hand into the nest at that moment, you might chance on the shell. But he himself had always missed the count.

The youngest of the nobles gave O Ji San more money that he had ever seen in his life and then sat gazing into the garden long after the swallows had twittered themselves to sleep.

The next morning he went to see the great lord on the hill. The lord was very gracious and they went down together to his kitchen. The lord commanded a scaffolding to be built to reach the thatch. By mid-day the carpenters had had tea three times and the scaffolding was ready. Twenty men were sent up to watch the swallows, but the birds swept out in desperate flight and would not come back.

The youngest of the nobles came sadly back to the inn and sent for O Ji San. He was still hopeful. 'Scared they were and small blame to them,' said he. 'Give them a night to settle down and then let one man go quietly up in a strong basket and watch them all day.'

The youngest of the nobles again sat gazing into the sunset while the frogs croaked in the pond. Next morning he sent up his trustiest servant to watch the swallows, but the man saw and found nothing all day.

The youngest of the nobles got into the basket himself and they pulled him up, not daring to laugh at his earnest face. He reached the darkness of the rafters where the swallows were settling to sleep. In one of the nests a swallow was turning round and round. Seven times he counted and slipped his hand softly into the nest and caught something hard and cold.

'Lower away!' he cried with a gay shout that brought the awakened swallows wheeling about his head. There was an answering shout from below – and then a cry of horror for, even as they began to lower the basket, the rope snapped and the youngest of the nobles crashed to the ground.

They took him up and laid him on the mats and dashed water on his face. In a little while he opened his eyes and asked for a candle. They brought it, wondering, and he tried to raise himself but could not.

'Show the shell to me,' he whispered, moving his clenched hand. They opened the fingers and held that which he grasped before his eyes. It was no shell, but

34

a smooth piece of clay. The youngest of the nobles shut his eyes.

They carried him broken to his palace among the hills. They asked him if he would have word sent to the Princess, but he forbade them under pain of death. 'At least,' he thought, '*she* shall not laugh at me.'

But a seller of mountain trout from the village at the foot of the Great Pass, came to the house of the Princess with his fish and told the cook the tale as they drank tea together. Thus it came to the Princess's maids and so to the Princess herself. When she heard it, she went to Taketori with a stricken face.

'You said I made a fool of him,' she cried, 'and I have sent him to his death. Bring me no more talk of men and marriages, my father.'

The Princess Splendour sat down and wrote to the youngest of the nobles and this is what she wrote:

Sir,

If tears could heal you, you were whole today.

The youngest of the nobles was already dying when her message arrived. Even so he begged one companion to hold the paper and another to steady the pen while he wrote:

Lady,

I have come to the Even Pass of Yomi, and am like, it seems, to go farther. Yet I go gladly since your pity follows me.

Even as he signed his name, he died. Thus ended the wooing of the youngest of the nobles.

The Emperor's Hunting Party

The Emperor sat in his Inner Apartment and drank tea out of pale yellow cups that made it gleam like gold. There were butterflies painted inside the cups and he watched them while he listened to the Lady Tassel who had charge of the Flowers of the Palace, as the young court beauties were called.

The Lady Tassel told him of the suitors for the hand of the Princess Splendour. The Emperor was amused and gave orders that she should be brought to see him; but she would not come for she said there were Flowers enough at the palace without her.

'Is it the bride of the Emperor she would be?' thought the Emperor. 'Absurd!' For all that it was absurd, he could not get her out of his mind, so after three months he sent for old Taketori.

Taketori came and fell upon his face.

'Go and inform your daughter that she is to be Empress of Japan,' said the Emperor. 'I have spoken. On the day you bring her to me, you shall be made a Knight of the Empire.'

The Princess sat very still while Taketori told her of the Emperor's will. 'What say you, daughter?' he asked at last.

'My father,' said the Princess quietly, 'I have told you that marriage is not for the fairy folk.'

Taketori begged her over and over again to listen to the Emperor's request, but she listened with her head turned away. 'Is it so great a thing that you should be a Knight of the Empire?' she asked.

Taketori looked at her beseechingly. 'It is the right to wear a sword,' he said longingly.

The Princess turned, smiling sadly. 'I will go to the Palace,' she said, 'but if any man should touch this hand of mine, all my radiance will vanish and I shall be changed into viewless air.'

Silenced and wondering, Taketori went back to the Palace. The Emperor heard him out. 'My lady is hard to win,' he said lightly. 'In three weeks' time I shall ride in a hunting party. It may be that I shall take a cup of wine with you.'

The day of the hunting party dawned clear with a fresh wind from the hills. 'It might be well,' said the Emperor, 'that a litter follow us. It may be that the boar will wound one of us before the sport ends.' He shook his bamboo spear and rode forward with his hundred knights.

Until the sun was high he rode with the party. Then, where a bridle-path struck off the road, climbing the hill among the bamboos, he paused. 'It is my will,' he said, 'to drink a cup of wine with my faithful subject, Taketori. He is an old man and I would not put him to the necessity for ceremony. Await me.' He threw the reins of his horse to an attendant and disappeared on foot among the bamboos.

The palace of the Princess Splendour stood empty and open to the sun. Taketori had gathered his retainers together and gone down to the main approach to receive the Emperor. Even the Princess's maids had run to the end of the garden and climbed the maple that overhung the valley so that they might see the hunting-party passing.

The great black gates were shut, but the tiny 'earthquake door' in them was open and the Emperor bowed his head and stepped through. Up the old stone entrance-way he passed, under the shadow of the pines and so into the quiet house. Room after room he passed through, sliding the screens behind him, until before him the paper screens of the Inner Apartment glowed like a shell. He slid them apart and looked within.

The Princess knelt at the dais, arranging iris in a great bowl. At the sliding of the screens, she turned her head and saw a huntsman standing there. She rose, a little afraid.

'Sir, have you lost your way?' she asked gently.

The Emperor stood silent, for he had seen her face.

Then the Princess saw the Chrysanthemum, the royal emblem, blazing on his shoulder. Hastily she threw her trailing sleeve across her face and turned away. The Emperor sprang forward and caught her other sleeve and they stood there, the long purple sleeve between them.

'Princess,' said the Emperor, 'I will not let you go.'

The Princess swayed to her knees, her face still hidden in the silken sleeve. 'Sire,' she said piteously, 'I pray you, leave me!'

'If I go, you go with me,' said the Emperor and he stooped and caught her. But even as he did so, his hands closed on viewless air. The room was empty and the radiance of the Princess gone.

The Emperor stood stricken, then he fell upon his knees. 'Princess, have pity!' he cried. 'Show me your face again and I swear by the honour of my divine ancestors, never to seek you more.'

Again the Princess appeared and her radiance shone about her. 'Sire,' she said, 'marriage is not for we fairy folk.'

'But love is,' said the Emperor, and bowed his head at her feet.

Swiftly the Princess went from him and the Emperor rose and passed out through the silent palace to where his company awaited him. But he hunted no more that day.

The Passing of the Princess

For three years the Emperor wooed the Princess Splendour, but he did not once see her face again. Taketori was made a knight, but never again did the Emperor come up the bridle-path through the bamboos to drink a cup of tea with him.

Morning by morning, a messenger knelt before the Princess with the Emperor's greetings for the day. Sometimes his token was a rare gem, but more often a flower that he had tended for her himself. The Court was very quiet in those days for, when the business of state was done, the Emperor withdrew to his own rooms and sat there gazing down the valley, or dreaming over the gold-splashed paper on which the Princess had made her answer.

For the Princess did make answer – very distant and humble at first, then with a glimmer of laughter, until their messages tilted back and forth as gaily as a shuttle-cock, weighted with the Emperor's heart.

When the spring of the third year came and the hills were purple with wisteria, a change came over the Princess. With each full moon she stole away to the upper verandah and sat there watching the moon rise over the mountains. Following, her maids would find their mistress kneeling in tears with hands outstretched. June came and, when the young moon showed clear, the Princess's grief could not be hidden. Night after night she watched it rounding and on the eve of the full moon she sought out Taketori.

'My father,' she said, 'with the full of the moon the time is come that I should go to the place from which I came.'

'Child,' said Taketori, 'you came from the bamboos.'

'I came from yonder,' said the Princess, and she pointed to where the moon hung over the valley. 'Tomorrow night they will come to take me back.'

'Who will dare to come?' asked the old man fiercely.

'The Moon-King, my father,' said the Princess sadly.

The old man fell at her feet and begged her not to leave him, and the Princess knelt down on the mats beside him to comfort him.

'My father,' she said, 'for three moons I have knelt

and prayed to the Moon-King to let me stay, but he will not hear. Tomorrow night at midnight, the moon-people will come for me.'

Then Taketori rose in a frenzy of grief. He sent word to the Emperor and the Emperor sent his own guards, two thousand strong, to guard the palace of the Princess. They ranked themselves at twilight, a thousand at the palisade and a thousand on the roof with their bows drawn. The Princess's maids put on their war-garments and stood before the Inner Apartment holding their bamboo spears. Inside sat the Princess, white and still in her old mother's arms, while Taketori paced up and down, his sword in his hand.

'No man can stand against the Emperor's archers,' said Taketori stoutly.

'The warriors of the moon cannot die,' said the Princess sadly, and even as she spoke the moon rose.

Silence fell on everyone. Slowly the moon swung up into the sky and the watchers held their breath.

From very far off there rang a bugle-call, faint and clear and high, and out of the moon poured a waterfall of glittering points of light. Down the steep places of the sky came a shining army, fair and terrible with banners. Their radiance lightened all the earth.

'Shoot!' cried Taketori, but the archers stood like dead men. Nearer came the host, halting at last about a man's height above the ground.

The ranks parted and their leader stood alone. So blinding was the light that shone about him that Taketori fell upon his face.

'Old man,' said the Moon-King, 'bring forth my daughter.'

'Sire,' said Taketori beseechingly, 'she has been *my* daughter for many years.'

'It is many years ago since the Princess was banished to this dim earth,' said the Moon-King, 'but her banishment is ended. Bring her forth.'

'Sire,' cried the old man desperately, 'she is ill . . .'

The Moon-King turned from him. 'Daughter!' he called.

Of their own accord the shutters, bolted and barred as they were, slid back. The Princess came slowly forward. She was weeping and tears rolled down her face.

'What are these?' asked the Moon-King curiously, watching the tears glitter in the light.

'I weep for sorrow,' said the Princess, 'for my desire is to stay here.'

'Fool!' said her father, the Moon-King, 'would you indeed live and suffer and die as these mortals?'

'If I might live their life, I would gladly die their death,' said the Princess.

The Moon-King turned and took a shining goblet from one of his followers. 'Drink!' he commanded.

The Princess drank the Elixir of Life and the watchers saw the liquid ripple like a golden light down her throat. Even as she drank, it was as though a dim veil fell from her and her beauty blazed even more fiercely upon them, dazzling their eyes.

'Now take this!' said the Moon-King and he held out the feathered robe which the Immortals wear when they pass from earth to heaven.

'Not yet,' said the Princess, 'for once I put it on, I shall not remember to be sorry any more. I have somewhat yet to do.'

She took the Elixir of Life and knelt before Taketori and O Ba San. 'Drink!' she said. 'Since I cannot stay to comfort you in your death, I would have you live for ever.'

'If you go,' cried old Taketori and his wife together, 'we pray the gods for death.'

The Princess passed swiftly into the Inner Apartment. There she knelt before her writing-table and, pouring the Elixir into a crystal bottle, she wrote her last message to the Emperor.

'Hasten!' cried the Moon-King sternly. 'We must away from this foul earth.'

Slowly the Princess rose and came to him, her face as pale as the moonlight. The Moon-King wrapped the feathered robe about her and led her to his chariot. She walked as one in a dream. Again the bugle blew, unbearably sweet, and the great company turned to climb the stairway of the sky. The shining army moved away, growing ever more distant, until at last it was nothing but glittering points of light. The bugle sounded again, clear and far away, and the gates of the moon swung open. As they closed the world was left in deep and utter darkness.

They brought the Emperor the crystal bottle and with it the Princess's letter. This is what it said:

My friend,

It is of your grace that you have kept one so ungracious in your august thoughts. Yet, though I could not share your life, I would have you share my immortality. Drink and remember that my last remembrance, before all things were forgotten, was of you.

The Emperor knelt to write his last letter to the Princess Splendour:

My Lady,

I will not drink, for to live is to remember, and memory is bitter pain.

Then he took the letter and the crystal bottle and sent for the highest officer of his court.

'Take these,' he ordered. 'Pour out the Elixir and burn the letter on the summit of the mountain that is nearest to heaven, the mountain of eternal snow. It may be that the smoke of the burning may reach her and she may for a moment remember.'

It was on Fuji-Yama that the deathless draught was poured. Some say that for this reason the mountain is called the Deathless Mountain, but others say that the name means 'No second', because the beauty of the Princess Splendour will never again have its like upon the earth.

Gillie Martin the Fox

A Story from
Scotland

ONCE upon a time there was a King and Queen who had one son, Ian by name. The Queen died and the King took a new Queen, and she had not much liking for MacIan. He made little sorrow for that, for he was every day and night hunting. There was not a bird that flew over his head that he could not bring down with his arrow and many were the deer that he killed. There was never a day that he went out and came home with his bag empty.

46

But one day he was out hunting and saw neither feather nor fur. There was not a bird in the air, nor so much as a rabbit in the wood. He was coming home, hungry and tired, with the empty bag on his shoulder, when a blue falcon came over his head. He heard the whirr of her wings and let fly an arrow, but it only grazed her wing. The blue falcon flew on and there fell but one blue feather. MacIan picked it up and put it in his bag.

'What sport had you today, MacIan?' asked his stepmother when she met him.

MacIan opened his hunting bag and showed her the blue feather in his hand. The Queen looked at it and knew it.

'Hear me, MacIan,' she said. 'I am setting you under spells and crosses that you be wet with rain and cold with wind and wearied with travel, until you bring me the bird that lost that feather.'

Then MacIan turned upon the Queen.

'And I,' said he, 'am setting you under spells and crosses that you shall stand with one foot on the great house, and one foot on the castle, and your face to the wind whichever way it blows, until I come again.'

Away he went to look for the falcon and the Queen was left standing with one foot on the great house, and one foot on the castle, and the north wind blowing in her face.

MacIan, he went off across the heather with the north wind blowing behind him and he was hungry and cold.

Night came and the small birds went to their beds, but there was no bed for MacIan. On he went till the darkness was thick and then he crept down behind a clump of briars for shelter. He was not long there when who should come by but Gillie Martin, the fox.

'You have a sorrowful face on you, MacIan,' said the fox, 'and indeed you come on a bad night. I have nothing myself but a sheep's trotter, and an old sheep too: but let that be.' He sat down beside Ian at the back of the briar, and they kindled a fire and roasted the trotter and spent the night together. In the morning Gillie Martin said, 'Is it a blue falcon you are after, MacIan?'

'It is so,' said MacIan.

'She lives with the Giant of the five heads and the five humps and the five throats. Myself can show you his house. And if you will take my advice, you will hire yourself to him for a serving-lad and you will look well after his hens. When he sees you ready and careful with the hens, he will maybe give you the falcon to feed. Be good to the falcon and when the giant is out of the house, take her and run: but don't let so much as one of her feathers touch anything in the house, or you will rue it.'

'I shall be careful,' said MacIan. So Gillie Martin took him to the Giant's house and then went off over the hill. MacIan rapped at the door.

'Who is that?' asked the Giant.

'Are ye wanting a serving-lad?' asked MacIan.

'What can you do?' said the Giant.

'I can feed the hens and gather the eggs and feed the

pigs and fodder the cows and milk the cows and the goats.'

'I am in need of a lad like yourself,' said the Giant and he hired him.

Now MacIan was good to all the creatures, but he was very good to the hens and the ducks. The ducks went behind him in a string all day long, and the hens grew fat under him. 'He is a fine lad,' said the Giant to himself. 'One hen in the pot today is as big as two before he came. I wonder might I trust him with the falcon to feed?'

He gave MacIan the falcon to feed and if MacIan was good to the hens, he was twice as good to the falcon. 'I wonder,' said the Giant to himself, 'might I leave him the falcon to keep if I went away for a day?' He gave MacIan the falcon to keep and away he went over the hill.

MacIan waited until he was out of sight and took the falcon on his fist. He opened the door and the falcon sat quiet, for she liked MacIàn. But when she saw the clear day she spread her wings and the tip of the longest feather touched the door post and the post screeched. Back came the Giant over the hill and caught MacIan.

'I will tell you what I was after,' said MacIan, and told him.

'Hear me now,' said the Giant. 'I will not give you my falcon till you bring me the White Sword of Light from the Big Women of Doura.'

Away went MacIan downhearted over the moors, and again he met Gillie Martin.

'You have a sorrowful face on you, MacIan,' said he. 'Well you may, as you did not do what I told you. It is a bad night tonight, for I have but a sheep's trotter. But let that be.'

They kindled a fire and roasted the trotter and MacIan slept till morning. Then they went down to the shore and looked at the sea.

'Yonder is the way to Doura,' said Gillie Martin. 'I will be a boat and you shall sail the seas in her until you come to Doura. Go to the Seven Big Women and hire yourself out: say you are fine at keeping steel and silver bright and shining, and maybe they will trust you with the White Sword of Light. But when you take it, beware that the sheath touches nothing inside the house or you will rue it.'

Then Gillie Martin turned himself into a boat and MacIan stepped in and took the oars and rowed across to Doura. He left the boat and went up the sands and knocked at the door. Out came the Seven Big Women.

'Are you wanting a lad?' asked MacIan.

'What can you do?' said the Seven Big Women.

'I am fine at polishing,' said MacIan.

'We were wanting a lad to do that,' said the Big Women and they hired MacIan. For six weeks he stayed and there was not a rusty nail in the house that he had not bright and shining. 'He is a good lad,' said the Seven Big Women. 'I wonder might we give him the polishing of the White Sword of Light?'

They gave it him and he polished it till it shone like a lightning flash and every day he was polishing it. Then one day the Seven Big Women went out and he slipped the Sword into its sheath and made out of the door. But the point of the sheath touched the doorstep and the doorstep screeched and back came the Seven Women running.

'I will tell you what I was after,' said MacIan, and told them.

'Indeed,' said they, 'you shall not have it, unless you bring us the Yellow Filly that belongs to the King of Erin.'

Down to the sea shore went MacIan and again Gillie Martin met him.

'You have a sorrowful face on you, MacIan,' said Gillie Martin. 'Well you may, as you did not do what I told you.' So they sat down together and MacIan slept till morning. When he awoke, Gillie Martin was sitting on his tail looking at the sea.

'Yonder's the road to Erin,' he said. 'I will be a boat and you shall sail to Erin and be stable lad to the King, and maybe he will give you charge of the Yellow Filly. But when you are taking her, mind that no part of her touches anything in the stable or you will rue it.'

They sailed across to Erin. Up went MacIan to the King's house and the gatekeeper asked him his business.

'Maybe,' said he, 'the King is in need of a stable lad?'

The King came out and looked at him. 'What can you do?' he asked.

'I can curry the horses and tend them and fodder them, and clean the bits and the harness rings.'

'I was wanting a lad to do that,' said the King.

For a while MacIan was in the stable and the King liked him well. The horses grew fat and their coats were sleek and the silver bits were shining. 'He shall have charge of the Yellow Filly,' said the King.

So MacIan had charge of the Yellow Filly. She liked him well and he did as he pleased with her. Her coat was as smooth as polished brass. She was so swift that she could leave the wind that was behind her and catch up the wind that was before her.

Then the King went hunting. 'Now is my time,' thought MacIan. He saddled the filly and bridled her and took her head to lead her out through the door. She was almost through when she switched her tail and it touched the post of the door. Screech went the post and back from the hunt came the King. When he heard what MacIan had to say, he said, 'Indeed, you shall not have her till you bring me the daughter of the King of France to be my wife.'

So down came MacIan to the shore of the Irish Sea, and again Gillie Martin met him and shared his fire and his meat with him. 'It is for France we are now!' he said. 'I will be a great ship and I will take you over, but once there you must shift for yourself.'

They came to France and Gillie Martin ran aground. 'Away now to the King's house!' said he. 'Tell him it is a King's son you are and your crew all drowned, and your ship run ashore. And bid him come and tell you how to get her off.'

Away went MacIan to the palace and told the King his story. The King of France and the Queen of France and the court came down to the shore to see the ship, and the King's daughter with them. And while they stood, there came from the ship the sweetest music that ever was heard.

'What is that?' asked the King of France's daughter.

'It is a harp I have,' said MacIan.

'I should like to see it,' said she, and she went on board and MacIan after her. She went down into the ship and the music kept ever before her. 'It must be on deck after all,' she said, but when she came up above she found that the ship was in the midst of the sea and blue water all around her.

'This is an ill trick, MacIan,' said the princess. 'Where are you taking me?'

'I am taking you to Erin,' said MacIan, 'for the King

wishes you to be his wife. Then he will give me his Yellow Filly so that I may give her to the Seven Big Women of Doura, so that they will give me the White Sword of Light, so that I may bring it to the Giant of the five heads and five humps and five throats, so that he will give me the blue falcon. Then shall I be able to give the blue falcon to my stepmother and be free from crosses and spells.'

'I have no wish to be wife to the King of Erin,' said the princess. 'I would rather be wife to yourself.'

MacIan was well pleased. They came to Erin and stepped on shore. At once Gillie Martin changed himself from a ship into a beautiful young woman. 'I will be wife to the King of Erin,' said Gillie Martin. 'Let the King of France's daughter wait here until we come again.'

Up to the King's palace went MacIan, with Gillie Martin walking beside him like a princess. The King came out and saw her and at once he gave MacIan the Yellow Filly, with a golden saddle on her back and a silver bridle on her head.

'Will you not wait for the feast?' said the King of Erin to MacIan.

'I am in great haste,' answered MacIan and he hurried down to the shore where the King of France's daughter awaited him.

All day Gillie Martin pretended to be the princess and the King of Erin made great joy of his wedding. But when evening came, Gillie Martin became Gillie Martin once again; he scratched the King with his four paws and away he ran to MacIan and the King of France's daughter.

'I will be a ship again,' said he. 'Get you on board before the King of Erin finds us.'

They sailed to the shore of Doura and again Gillie Martin became Gillie Martin. 'I will be the Yellow Filly,' he said. 'Put the silver bridle on my head and give me to the Seven Big Women and await you here. It may be they will soon tire of riding.'

Up to the house went MacIan with Gillie Martin pacing beside him as the Yellow Filly. Out ran the Seven Big Women with the White Sword of Light in their hands. MacIan took it away to where he had left the King of France's daughter and the Yellow Filly. The Seven Big Woman were well pleased with the Yellow Filly *they* had got and were in a hurry to ride her. Up they got on her back, one after another, till all the seven were upon her. Off went Gillie Martin over the moors of Doura and up to the top of the mountain where it goes down sharp to the sea. There he stopped with his two fore feet on the edge of the cliff. Then he lifted his heels and over went the Seven Big Women. Away went Gillie Martin laughing.

'Come now,' said he; 'I will be a boat again. Get you all on board and we will go back to Scotland.'

On the shores of Scotland, Gillie Martin said, 'I will be the Sword of Light. Come with me to the Giant. It may be he will soon have enough of swords.'

When the Giant saw MacIan coming, he ran and put the blue falcon in a basket and gave it to him. Then he took Gillie Martin into his hand and went into his hall. There he pranced about, sweeping the sword this way and that way, until Gillie Martin was dizzy. So Gillie Martin swung himself about and swept off the Giant's five heads and that was the end of him.

Away went Gillie Martin to MacIan and said, 'Hear me, get you on the Yellow Filly with the King of France's daughter behind you, and let her hold the basket with the blue falcon. And do you ride home with the Sword of Light in your hand and its back against your nose. For if you ride not so, the Queen will see you coming and she will give you a look out of her eye that will turn you into a bundle of sticks. But if the back of the Sword is to your nose and she sees the glancing edge, it is herself will be turned into a bundle of sticks.'

Then Gillie Martin sat down on his tail and watched them out of sight. MacIan rode until he saw the glen and the Queen standing with one foot on the great house and one foot on the castle. When she saw him, she gave him a look, but the edge of the Sword of Light turned it back upon her and she became a bundle of sticks.

So now MacIan had the best wife in Scotland, and a horse so swift that it could leave the wind that was behind it and catch the wind that was before it, and the blue falcon to keep him in sport when hawking, and the White Sword of Light for a battle. There was no more trouble from the Queen and MacIan was well pleased.

Then said he to Gillie Martin, 'Hear me ! Go through my land and welcome; and take any sheep and welcome; for never an arrow will my servants shoot at you or at any of your kind. Take what you will.'

'Keep your flocks, MacIan,' said Gillie Martin. 'There are more than you that have sheep, and I will get my fill in another place without putting trouble on my friends.'

And the fox, Gillie Martin, went over the hill.

And so the story is ended.

The Adventures of Hasan
of El Basra

A Story from
Arabia

How Hasan Journeyed with Bahram the Persian
to the Mountain of the Clouds

In the city of Basra there once lived a young goldsmith
whose name was Hasan. He was a handsome young
man, and generous. To him there came one day a Persian who watched him as he blew the charcoal with the
bellows and hammered out the gold.

'My son,' said the Persian, 'I can teach you a better and an easier way to make gold.'

'What is that, O my master?' asked the young man, for the Persian appeared to be an old and wise man.

'Many have asked me for the secret and I have refused to tell them,' said the Persian, 'but I will tell you for I have no son of my own and you please me.'

'When will you tell me the secret?' asked the young man.

'Tomorrow I will come and show you how to make pure gold from copper,' said the Persian and he went away.

Hasan went home amazed, but when he told his mother of the Persian's promise, she said, 'Beware of listening to Persians, my son, for they are a cunning people and they like to plot evil against the faithful.'

'Peace, O my mother!' said Hasan. 'This Persian is a wise old man and kindly.'

On the next day the Persian came. 'Give me a piece of copper,' he said, and Hasan gave him a broken copper plate. The Persian cut it into pieces, threw them into the crucible and blew the fire until they melted. Then he took a paper filled with a yellow powder and sprinkled the contents into the crucible. At once the molten copper became pure gold! This he gave to Hasan who took it to the market and sold it for fifteen thousand pieces of silver.

Hasan took the silver home to his mother, but she shook her head, saying evil would come of it. Nevertheless Hasan went back to the Persian and besought him to reveal the secret. 'I cannot teach you except in my own house,' said the Persian.

Hasan went with him and the Persian made a feast for him, and promised to marry him to his daughter and to teach him all the art of making gold, and Hasan rejoiced.

'Taste this sweetmeat,' said the Persian, 'for it is very rare.' Hasan did so and at once he fell into a swoon. 'I have you, O dog of the Arabs!' cried the Persian and he put Hasan into a great chest and had him carried to the harbour. There the Persian went on board a ship and took with him the chest holding Hasan.

When Hasan came to himself, he was lying on deck in the midst of the sea with the Persian sitting beside him.

'Oh my father!' he said, 'what have you done to me?'

'Dog!' said the Persian. 'I have slain nearly a thousand youths like you and you shall make the thousandth.'

He called for a brazier and knelt before it and said to Hasan, 'This is the Fire that is my god: worship it with me and I will marry you to my daughter and give you half my wealth.'

'Never!' said Hasan boldly. 'You are an infidel.'

For a long time the Persian tormented Hasan, but still he would not worship the fire. At last the sailors told the Persian they would kill him if he did not cease his tormenting of such a likable young man.

Then the Persian changed his ways and swore to him

that he had only been doing these things to try his courage. He gave Hasan silk robes and spoke kindly to him and Hasan forgave him his cruelty.

When six months were ended, the ship came to anchor off a strange shore covered with pebbles, white and yellow and blue and black. Here the Persian landed with Hasan and went inland into the desert.

When they were out of sight of the ship, the Persian sat down and took a copper drum and beat upon it. At once a dust arose far off in the desert. Hasan was afraid, but the Persian said : 'Fear not, my son, we go to the Mountain of Clouds where is the elixir which changes copper to gold. Help me and you shall share its secret.'

The dust cloud came nearer and Hasan saw that it was made by three camels running swiftly. The Persian got upon one, Hasan on another and on the third they put their food. For seven days they travelled until they reached a green dome standing on four pillars of red gold and there they descended to eat and drink, and the camels disappeared.

A great way off Hasan saw the shining of a palace roof. 'O my father, what is that?' he asked.

'It is the palace of the Devils,' answered the Persian. He beat the drum and three camels appeared and they rode on for another seven days.

On the morning of the eighth day the Persian said, 'O Hasan, what do you see?'

'I see a mist between the east and the west,' said Hasan.

'That is not mist,' said the Persian, 'but a great mountain on which the clouds divide. On that mountain we shall find what I desire. The yellow powder which turns copper to gold is made from a herb that grows upon that mountain. You shall get it for me and I will show you all my art.'

'It is well,' replied Hasan, but he had no hope now of his life and repented that he had not heeded his mother's warning against the Persian.

They came to the foot of the mountain which was so steep that no man could climb it. There the Persian halted and made a fire and baked three cakes. Then he beat the drum and when the camels came he killed one of them and stripped off its skin.

'Now, my son,' he said, 'get into this skin and take with you the cakes and the bottle of water and I will sew up the skin. Great birds, called rocs, will think you are a dead camel and will carry you to their home on the top of the mountain. Take this knife with you and when they have set you down, rip open the skin and the birds will fly away. Then call down to me and I will tell you what you must do.'

Even so did Hasan and the rocs came and carried him to the top of the mountain. He cut the skin open and came out and called to the Persian at the foot of the mountain. The Persian danced for joy and cried out, 'Turn round and tell me what is behind you.'

When Hasan turned, he saw piles of strange-coloured wood and beside them the white bones of men, so he told the Persian all he had seen.

'Throw me down six bundles of the wood,' shouted

the Persian, 'for the yellow powder is made from the ashes of its burning.'

Hasan did as he was bid, but to his horror the Persian cried, 'I have had all I want of you, dog of the Arabs! Lay your bones with those others, or throw yourself down—I care not.' He beat the drum and set off over the desert with his camels.

Then Hasan despaired of his life. He walked round the mountain but on three sides it fell sheer to the desert. Only on the fourth side was the sea, and every wave of it a great mountain. Here Hasan recited part of the Koran and repeated the funeral prayer, then he cast himself down into the sea, expecting to be drowned.

But he was not drowned and after some hours the sea cast him on to the sand. Hasan gave thanks and was glad.

He walked a long time, looking for something to eat, until he saw a palace before him at the edge of the desert. It was the palace of the Devils. He went on and all about him was the sound of running water and the shadow of gardens. He entered a doorway and saw two damsels like two fair moons seated on the marble floor of the hall. There was a chessboard between them and they were playing a game.

At last one of the damsels lifted her head and saw him and, so kind was her look, that Hasan told her all his story. She took him by the hand and said, 'Weep not, for you shall be our brother.' They brought him clothes and set bread and fruit before him and comforted him.

They told him that they were two of seven sisters, daughters of one of the Kings of the Jinn. Their father was jealous lest any man should see their beauty, so he had sent them to this palace at the edge of the desert. Here they lived alone and every day five of them went out to hunt in the desert and two stayed at home to cook and keep the house.

Even as they spoke, the five sisters came in from the desert and they also said that Hasan should be their brother.

So Hasan lived with the seven princesses a full year and they were happy together.

The Palace at the Edge of the Desert

There came a day when the sisters saw a great cloud of dust rising in the desert and they hid Hasan in his room telling him that the King, their father, had sent messengers and he must not be seen. Then came troops of horsemen, riding towards the palace like the waves of the sea. The King had a longing to see his daughters and had sent for them.

The princesses came to take leave of Hasan. 'It will be two moons before we come back,' they said, 'but the palace is yours and here are the keys of every room. But one door, O our brother, we pray you not to open!' They showed him the forbidden door and then they departed with their father's troops.

Hasan was very lonely without the princesses. He went hunting in the desert and caught game and cooked it, but it had no taste because he ate alone. He wandered through the palace and at last he came upon the door which the princesses had forbidden him to open. Having nothing else to do, he felt a great desire to open it and, after a time, he did so.

Through the door was a flight of steps which led him to the roof of the palace and there, to his astonishment, was a great garden with the shade of trees and pleasant alleys and the singing of birds. So high was he that he could see, far off, the green of corn-lands and the blue shining of the sea. One of the alleys led him to a pavilion of jacinth and emerald and a pool of clear water paved with precious stones, and above it a trellis of sandalwood.

Here Hasan sat down. Lifting his head he saw ten white birds flying over the desert and coming towards the palace. 'It is the pool they seek,' he thought to himself, and hid lest they should see him and be startled. The birds came nearer and he saw that they were like swans but larger. They perched on the edge of the pool and it seemed to him that one of them was queen over the rest.

A little while they rested; then casting their white plumage from them, they stepped into the pool. Hasan saw in amazement they had changed into young maidens. Beautiful as they were, their queen was even more lovely and she moved like the bending of willows. For a while they swam in the pool, laughing with one another, but afterwards put on their white plumage again and flew away over the desert. Then Hasan returned to his room, but for days he neither ate nor drank for he could not forget the beauty of the queen.

Again there rose a dust in the desert and the seven princesses came home.

'O our brother,' they cried, 'what is the matter? You are thin and worn.'

For a long time he would not tell them, but at last he confessed that he had opened the forbidden door.

'Alas our brother!' they cried. 'You have seen her and there is no hope for you, for she is the daughter of the King of the Kings of the Jinn and under his awful power there are Enchanters and Sages and Diviners and Devils and Marids. He has seven daughters and it is the youngest and fairest with whom you have fallen in love. They rule over seven islands and it is death for a stranger to be found near them. Put the memory of her from you and be comforted.' But Hasan could not.

In a little while they rode off on a twenty-day hunting party, but Hasan did not go with them and the youngest of the princesses stayed to take care of him. When her sisters had gone, she came to Hasan and said, 'Be of good cheer, O my brother, for I have thought of a plan. When the daughter of the King of the Kings of the Jinn comes again on the first day of the new moon, hide yourself on the roof garden. When she is playing in the pool with her maids, steal her white plumage and she will not be able to fly home again."

It happened even so. Hasan hid amongst the shrubs and the swans came flying over the desert. When they

were bathing in the pool, he stole the white plumage
and waited. When the Jinn's daughter came out of the
water, she gave a great cry, 'My swan plumage is lost
and I shall never see the islands again.'

Her maids stayed with her weeping, till it grew towards sunset when they must leave her. Putting on their

swan plumage, they departed, crying mournfully, and left their Princess alone on the roof. Hasan lifted her in his arms and carried her down to the palace and called his youngest sister. 'Go to her,' he begged, 'speak gently to her, for she is very frightened.'

So the youngest princess went to her and comforted her, and told the Swan Princess that it was a mortal who had done this for love of her. She gave her a room to herself in the palace and the strange Princess was comforted, but to Hasan she would not say a word.

When the other sisters came home from the hunt, they made much of the Swan Princess and she laughed with them and forgot to grieve. They begged her to speak graciously to Hasan and she relented, for she could not in her heart be angry with him when his love for her was so great.

'You have caught a bird from the air,' she said to him, 'and yet you desire to make her your wife!'

'O mistress of all beauty!' he said. 'My only desire is to be your slave till the end of the world. Come with me to the city of Baghdad and I will give you all that your heart can wish. There is no country better than my country and its people are good people.'

In a little while she consented to marry him and the seven sisters made a great feast which lasted for forty days, and everyone was happy.

At the end of the forty days, Hasan saw his mother in a dream and she had grown sad and old, for she thought him dead. In the morning he told his wife and his sisters and they bade him go to her. They beat the drum and a troop of camels came. The sisters loaded them with all manner of riches and Hasan and the Princess rode away. So at last they came to the door of his mother's house in the city of El Basra.

Great was her joy and she marvelled at the beauty of the Princess his wife. Then Hasan took ship with all that he had and they sailed up the Tigris to Baghdad. There he bought a palace, with gardens by the river, where he dwelt happily with his wife and his mother. For three years they lived in delight and the Princess had two sons.

How the Princess His Wife Went from Him in the Plumage of a Bird

Now at the end of the three years, Hasan remembered the seven princesses in the palace at the edge of the desert, and was grieved that he had broken his promise to visit them once every year. So he bought them presents, strange jewels and strange fruits, and gave his wife into the care of his mother.

'Know, O my mother,' he said, 'that she is the daughter of the King of the Kings of the Jinn, and the dearest thing that he has. The feather dress by which I captured her is hidden in a golden chest under the floor of the arbour of pomegranates. Let her not look upon it for she is a bird of the air and, if the desire of it came to her, she would fly from me and I should die of sorrow.'

Then he took leave of his wife and sons and went out beyond the city and beat the drum and, when the camels came, he departed over the desert.

For three days the Princess, his wife, was content, but soon she became weary of the house and the gardens and the flowing river, for she was lonely without Hasan.

'O my mother,' she said, 'take me to the Bath that I may see new faces.'

For a long time Hasan's mother would not consent, but the Princess coaxed her sweetly and she agreed to take her to the Bath. There the Princess took off her veil and all the women gazed upon her and gave thanks to Allah for her beauty.

There she was seen by a slave girl of Haroun al Raschid, Prince of the Faithful, who returned to the palace full of wonder.

'O my mistress,' she said to the Lady Zubeydeh, 'I have seen a woman, the loveliest ever created.' The Lady Zubeydeh was curious and sent her chamberlain to command Hasan's mother and wife to come to the palace.

Hasan's mother feared greatly, but the word of the palace must be obeyed. So she and the Princess embarked at the river gate and were brought to the secret gate of the palace garden and so to the Lady Zubeydeh. The Princess took off her veil and the palace was lit with her beauty.

'Now Allah be praised for your fairness!' exclaimed the Lady Zubeydeh. 'You are a delight to the eyes!'

'O my mistress,' said the Princess, 'there is one dress

71

that I have that is most beautiful and strange, for it is the plumage of a swan.'

'Send for it,' said the Lady, 'and wear it for us.'

'My husband and my husband's mother have the keeping of it,' said the Princess.

The Lady Zubeydeh begged Hasan's mother to bring the feather dress, but she would not, even though the Lady Zubeydeh offered her a necklace of jewels worth the treasure of the Persian Kings. Then they searched the old woman forcibly and found the key of the arbour where the dress was hidden and the chamberlain was sent to bring it. Hasan's mother wept and rent her clothes for she knew evil would come of it.

In a little while the chamberlain returned with the feather dress and gave it to the Princess. She put it on and flew softly about the garden, flying low like a swallow, and the women of the palace cried out with wonder at the strangeness of it and the shining of the feathers.

When the Princess felt the joy of the sun and the swift flowing of the wind through her feathers, the desire came upon her to see once again the home and the faces of her people, and to gaze once more upon the blueness of the sea about the islands. She flew higher and the Lady Zubeydeh looked up, shading her eyes, and cried: 'Excellent! But return now, O fairest among women!'

'There is no returning,' said the Princess; but when she saw Hasan's mother mourning, she was distressed because she knew that the old woman loved her.

'O my mother,' she said, 'I shall be lonely without

you. When my husband returns and he is stirred by longing for me, bid him come to me in the Islands of Wak-wak.'

She rose high into the air and, spreading her wings, she flew away to her own country.

How Hasan Journeyed to the Islands of Wak-wak

For three months Hasan stayed with his sisters, the princesses, in the palace at the edge of the desert, and they had much joy together. Then he returned to Baghdad.

When he entered his house, he found it empty and desolate, and his mother worn with weeping. When she told him what had happened, he was speechless for many hours. Then he mounted his camel and returned to the palace at the edge of the desert. His sisters were astonished to see him back so soon.

'O my sisters,' he said, 'my love has again become a bird of the air and is gone to her own people.' And they wept with him.

'Tell me, where are the Islands of Wak-wak?' asked Hasan, but his sisters could not tell him.

Said the eldest of the sisters: 'Let us send for my uncle, for he is wise.' She threw incense upon the fire, naming her uncle's name, and in a little while there arose a dust in the desert and in the midst of it, riding upon an elephant, was her uncle.

'Why did you send for me, O my niece?' he asked,

but when he heard Hasan's story, the old man was grieved for him.

'O my son,' he said, 'think no more of seeking her. You could not reach the Islands of Wak-wak even if the Flying Jinn and the wandering stars came to help you, for between the Islands and you are seven valleys, and seven seas, and seven mountains exceeding high. Return home and weary not your heart.'

'Nevertheless,' said Hasan, 'I will go.'

'Verily, you are a brave young man!' said the old man. 'Come with me.' He set Hasan behind him upon the elephant and for three days and three nights they rode over the desert until they came to a vast blue mountain. The stones on it were blue and in it was a door of iron. Leaving the elephant behind, Hasan and the old man went through the door into a great cavern. After a mile the cavern turned sharply and there were two great doors of brass. Through one of these the old man went alone and came back to Hasan leading a horse saddled and bridled. So swift was the horse that when he galloped the dust of the desert could not overtake him. Hasan mounted and the old man led him through the second brass door, beyond which was a vast desert.

'O my son,' he said, 'for ten days this horse will carry you over the desert. He will stop at the entrance to a cave. Let him go in but go not yourself until five days have passed. On the sixth day, an old man will come to you who is the chief of us all. Tell him your story and he will help you, but you would be wiser to return home and find a better wife than the one you have lost.'

'I will never go back until I find her,' said Hasan.

Then the old man gave him a letter to give to the chief and blessed him and departed.

For ten days Hasan flashed through the desert on the back of his horse and the wild horses of the desert raced with him. On the tenth day they came to the entrance to the cave and the horse went in, But Hasan waited for another five days.

On the sixth day a venerable old sheikh, clad in black, came out and Hasan knelt before him and gave him the letter. The old sheikh took it and went back into the cavern and for five more days Hasan waited anxiously. On the sixth day at dawn, the old sheikh came again, but this time clad in white. He spoke kindly to Hasan and brought him into the cavern to a great hall of marble and gold where fountains played and orange trees grew. There sat four aged men with incense-burners before them, each reading aloud from a book.

'My son,' said the sheikh, 'tell the company your story.' Hasan did so and they exclaimed when they heard it.

'Be wise, O young man, turn back,' they counselled. 'It is death to be found in the Islands of Wak-wak.'

'Do but help me to get there!' entreated Hasan. Then the sheikh struck the floor and called the Flying Jinn, and he appeared.

'O my son,' said the sheikh, 'mount on the shoulders of Dahnash the Flyer and he will take you to the heights of Heaven. To the Land of Camphor he will carry you, to whose King give this letter.'

Then Dahnash the Flyer rose with him into the upper air until, so high was he, he could hear the singing of the Angels in Heaven. In the dawn of the next day the Flyer set him down in a white clean land, shining and clear like camphor. For ten days he travelled till he came to the gate of a city. The keepers of the gate brought him to the King who read his letter and thought upon it for three days.

'My son,' he said, 'I will help you. In the harbour is a ship from the Islands of Wak-wak. I will give you into the care of the ship's master and he will hide you in a great chest and set you on land at the first of the Islands. These Islands are guarded by an army of women and no man may dare set foot there, so I know not what will befall you thereafter.'

For ten days Hasan was at sea, hidden in the great chest. On the eleventh day he was put on shore with cases of silk, balm and perfumes, and there the sailors left him.

At sunset Hasan saw an army come down from the hills: women in shining armour, terrible as locusts. They opened the cases and spread out the silks, but one woman stayed apart. She was old and seemed to be their leader. To her Hasan crept in the darkness and kissed her feet, crying, 'Have mercy upon me, O my mistress.'

Now the old warrior was wise. She made no stir but bade him wait until the other women had gone to their tents. Then she listened to Hasan's story and wept for pity. In the morning she gave him a coat of mail and veiled his face as if he were one of the women of the army, and she promised to take him to the Queen of the Innermost Isle who would help him to find his wife.

The Queen of the Innermost Isle was the Queen Noor-el-Huda, the eldest of the daughters of the King of the Kings of the Jinn, and the old woman was a favourite with her because she had nursed her and all her sisters. So, when the old woman went in to her, she kissed her and seated her by her side on the divan.

'O my mistress,' said the old woman, 'I have a strange tale to tell you," and she told her the tale of Hasan from beginning to end.

Then the Queen arose in fury. 'O worthless woman,' she cried, 'to bring a man into the Islands of Wak-wak, where never man has been! If it were not that you were my nurse, I would kill you and him with tortures. Bring him before me so that I may question him.'

The old woman, shaking with fear, brought in Hasan. The Queen sat upon the divan, veiled so that Hasan saw only her eyes.

'Who are you?' asked the Queen. 'From what country have you come?'

'O Queen of the Age,' said Hasan, 'my name is Hasan the Mournful, and I am of the city of El Basra.'

'It is said that your wife was a damsel from the Islands of Wak-wak. What was her name?' asked the Queen.

'I know not her name,' said Hasan, for indeed it was true.

'What did she say when she flew into the air?' asked the Queen.

77

'She said to my mother, "When my husband returns and is stirred with longing for me, bid him come to me in the Islands of Wak-wak."'

For a long while the Queen said nothing. At last she raised her head.

'I will have pity on you,' she said, 'I will not put you to death. Every damsel in my island shall pass before you and if one of them is your wife, I will give her to you. If not, I shall know you for a liar and I shall put you to death.'

All the damsels of the islands passed before Hasan, but his wife was not amongst them. Then the old woman said, 'O Queen of the Age, suffer him to see the damsels of the palace.'

Then the damsels of the palace passed before Hasan, but his wife was not amongst them. The Queen was enraged and raised her voice to call for the tormentors, but the old woman prostrated herself and said, 'O Queen, one face he has not seen.'

'Whose face is that?' asked the Queen.

'Your own,' said the old woman.

Then the Queen laughed and, turning to Hasan, she unveiled her face. When he saw it he gave a great cry and fell in a swoon.

'Verily,' said the Queen, 'he has lost his wits.'

At last Hasan came to himself. 'By Allah, O Queen,' he cried, 'either you are my wife or you are the person most like her in the world!'

'And how am I like her?' asked the Queen.

'In the brow which is like the new moon, and in the

mouth which is as the seal of Solomon,' said Hasan.

The Queen was well pleased and sent Hasan away with fair words, promising to seek his wife for him.

'O my mother,' said the Queen to her nurse, 'there is but one of my sisters who is like me in these things, and that is my youngest sister, the Princess Menar-es-Sena. Was it for this reason that she was so long absent from the Islands of Wak-wak, think you?'

'It is even so,' said the old woman.

'Go to her,' said the Queen, 'and tell her that I long greatly after her, for it is four years since she visited me. But say nothing to her of her husband.'

'O my mistress,' said the old woman, delighted, 'is it your purpose to bring them together in your tenderness of heart?'

'It is even so,' said the Queen, smiling, but there was wickedness and cruelty in her smile. 'Tell her to send her children first and to follow after herself.'

In seven days the old woman returned, bringing with her the two children.

'Now,' said the Queen, 'bring Hasan to me so that I may see whether the children are his or not.'

When Hasan came into the Queen's chamber, his two sons sat playing at the foot of her divan. They looked up and knew him and ran to him crying, 'O our father!'

Then the Queen rose up in fury and tore them from him and called her slaves. They dragged Hasan from the palace and threw him beyond the city walls and he lay there stunned. Meantime the Queen sat planning in what way she could torment her sister, the old woman crouched in the corner and wept, and the children cried for their father and would not be comforted.

The next day the Princess Menar-es-Sena came to the palace and was united with her children, her sister being hidden behind a curtain. The children ran to their mother, crying, 'Where is our father?' and she caught them and kissed them and cried bitterly. 'Have you seen your father?' she said. 'Would that I had never left him! If I knew where to find him, I would take you to him.'

Then the Queen, Noor-el-Huda, came out from behind the curtain.

'O wicked woman to marry a son of Adam, and you a daughter of the King of the Kings of the Jinn!' she cried bitterly. 'Dearly shall you suffer for it.'

She called her slaves and had her sister bound hand and foot and scourged. Then she left her in a swoon. None dared help the Princess, for though all hated the Queen for her cruelty, they feared her also.

How Hasan Came Back to Baghdad, the Abode of Peace

When Hasan came to himself, he was on the sea shore, beyond the walls of the city. There he wandered for a long time, full of sorrow. On a sudden he heard the voices of children quarrelling. It was two boys and they were fighting over a cap with strange signs upon it, and a carved brass rod.

'What ails you, my sons?' asked Hasan.

They dropped the rod and the cap and ran to him.

'Sir,' they cried, 'choose between us. Our father was one of the great enchanters. He is dead now and has left us these two things – but each of us wants the rod.'

'Why?' asked Hasan.

'Because whoever strikes the ground with the rod can call up the Kings of the seven tribes of the Jinns and they will serve him.'

'And what of the cap?'

'Whoever wears the cap will become invisible and can go wherever he pleases. Choose between us – which shall have the rod?'

Then Hasan took a stone and threw it a great way off.

'Run,' he said, 'and the first at the stone shall have the rod.' They ran, and when they were gone Hasan took the rod and put the cap on his head. He wished himself in the palace so that he might see his children and in a moment he was in the Queen's private room. The children sat on the divan crying and on the floor lay their mother, bound and in a swoon.

Then Hasan knew his wife and cried out so loudly that he brought her out of her swoon. He plucked the cap from his head and she saw him and forgot her pain.

Then she remembered. 'Oh my Lord,' she cried, 'go, before my sister returns and finds you here.'

'O Queen of every queen,' said Hasan, 'I will not go unless I take you with me.'

The Princess smiled sadly. 'There is no deliverance for me but in dying,' she said. 'Save yourself and leave me here.'

Even as she spoke, the Queen came back, but Hasan put on his cap and she did not see him. Again the Queen tormented her sister and again departed.

'O my lord,' said the Princess, 'do not grieve. This has befallen me because I left you.'

'Nay,' said Hasan, 'it was my fault, for it was I who left you alone in the first place.' He comforted her until the slaves came in, when he became invisible once more.

Night came down and all in the palace slept. Then Hasan came back to his wife and untied the cords that bound her. He took the older boy in his arms and she the younger, and they stole through the palace to the great door. It was shut and barred! The Princess began to cry softly and Hasan was in despair, but a voice was heard on the other side of the door. It was the old woman.

'O Princess,' she said, 'promise me that, if I open the door, you will take me with you.'

They promised and the door opened. 'Now,' said the old woman to Hasan, 'have you forgotten your rod?'

Hasan struck the rod on the ground. At once there rose before him the seven Kings of the Jinn, black and fearful, their heads among the stars and their feet in the roots of the earth. They kissed the ground at Hasan's feet as they bowed before him.

'I command you that you carry me and my wife and this virtuous woman to the city of Baghdad,' said Hasan.

82

The seven Kings of the Jinn said, 'O my master, we lived in the days of Solomon, Son of David, and he made us swear that we would carry none of the sons of Adam on our backs, but we will bring you three horses of the Jinn. They will carry you over thirsty deserts and terrible wastes and it may be that the people of the Islands will come after you, but we will fight for you.'

Hasan and the Princess mounted the horses of the Jinn and the old woman and the children with them. All that night they journeyed through the desert and for thirty days. On the thirty-first day they saw a great dust behind them and the Princess said fearfully, "It is the troops of the Island of Wak-wak.'

Then Hasan struck the ground with his rod and the seven Kings of the Jinn appeared before him.

'Fight these troops for us,' commanded Hasan and the seven Kings rejoiced. Then they went to the plain with their nine and forty tribes of Jinns and Devils and Marids, Flyers and Diviners and Enchanters. For two days they fought the troops of the Queen Noor-el-Huda in dust and crying and tempest. By the end of the second day, all the troops were slain and she herself was taken captive.

They brought her to Hasan and the Princess where they sat on divans of alabaster and ivory and gold.

'Behold!' said Hasan to the Princess, 'she who tortured you is in your power. Do with her as you will.'

Then the Princess Menar-es-Sena rose and kissed her sister and wept and unloosed her bonds. Then the Queen repented of what she had done and they sent her to her own country, and the old nurse with her, on two swift horses of the Jinn.

Hasan and the Princess continued their journey. They passed through the Land of Camphor and gave rich presents to the King. In the marble hall in the desert they found the aged sheikh among the orange trees and gave him the cap of invisibility for his kindness. They met the old man, the princesses' uncle, riding on his elephant and gave him the brass rod. And so at last they saw the green dome on pillars of red gold and beyond it the green palace and the pool and far off the Mountain of Clouds. Then Hasan wept for joy.

For ten days they stayed with the seven princesses who made much of Hasan and the Princess and the two children; then they continued their journey over the desert. For two months they journeyed and so came to Hasan's house with its private door opening on the desert. When Hasan knocked and his old mother heard his voice, she swooned for very joy. To the end of their days they lived in wealth and delight in Baghdad, the Abode of Peace.

The Crock of Gold

A Story from
Ireland

THERE was once a farmer's son, Tom Fitzpatrick, as fine and upstanding a young fellow as you'd find anywhere in Ireland. It was a holiday and there was a dance at the cross-roads. Tom knew that the prettiest girls in the countryside would be there, so he put on his Sunday clothes and set out to join them.

As he walked round the edge of the field, he heard a sharp little click in the hedge. 'Sure and it's too late for a stone-chat?' he thought and stopped to look amongst the bushes.

There in a hollow amongst the ripe blackberries was a tiny man only the height of your knee, sitting on a three-legged stool and hammering heels on a pair of shoes with silver buckles. Tom didn't need to be told who the little man was, for every Irishman knows a Leprechaun when he sees one and knows too that a Leprechaun has a crock of gold hidden away somewhere.

'God bless the work,' he said.

'Thank you kindly,' said the Leprechaun.

'It is a wonder to see you working and it being a holiday,' said Tom.

'That's as it may be,' said the Leprechaun and he took a drink from a little pitcher beside him.

'It's dry work making shoes,' said Tom.

'It is that same,' said the Leprechaun.

'What might it be in the pitcher?' asked Tom.

'Good Irish beer,' said the little man.

'Where did you get that?' asked Tom.

'I brewed it myself,' said the Leprechaun, looking at Tom over the top of the pitcher.

'Will you give me a taste of it?' asked Tom and he came a little nearer.

'Look to your father's corn!' said the Leprechaun quickly. 'It's destroyed it will be if you don't drive away the cows.'

Tom jumped and was just about to turn round when he remembered the ways of leprechauns. Take your eye off them and they whip out of sight. 'You'll not catch me out that way!' he said and grabbed the little fellow by the tail of his green coat.

'Now,' he said very fiercely, 'take me to your crock of gold, wherever it is you have hidden it, or I'll not be letting you go this side of Christmas.'

The Leprechaun was frightened. He swore he had no crock of gold, but Tom wasn't to be put off by that. The little man twisted and turned and tried all the tricks he knew to make Tom look elsewhere, but it was all no good. Tom was determined not to let him go, for a crock of gold he would have. Why, he could buy that plot of land near his father's fields and marry pretty Molly Maloney! He shook the Leprechaun until he cried out for mercy and at last gave in.

'Bad luck to you, I'll show you where I've hidden my gold,' he said. 'It's not very far away, but I warn you it's rough walking. I fear it'll be hard on your Sunday clothes.'

Tom all but looked down at his clothes, but, just in time, he remembered not to take his eyes off the Leprechaun.

'Lead the way and no more havering,' he said as fiercely as he could. Off went the little man and Tom after him, his eyes fixed on the fellow's back. Small as he was, the Leprechaun could keep up a good pace and he led Tom through every thorn bush and scraped him through every hedge and splashed him through every boggy patch, until Tom's best clothes weren't fit to be seen. But never once did he take his eyes off the Leprechaun.

'We're near it now,' said the Leprechaun at last. They had come out into the twenty-acre field. It was full of fine yellow ragwort which glowed fierily in the sunset. The Leprechaun walked a little way into it and stopped under a ragwort plant about twice the size of himself. There he stood in his green coat and said, 'Dig under this, and you'll find my own crock of gold. It's well dug in so it's a pity you haven't a spade.'

'That'll not be bothering me,' said Tom. 'I'll soon get one.' He thought of the field of yellow ragwort stretched so far around him. 'But how shall I know which plant to dig under when I come back?' he wondered. 'Sure, I must mark the right one somehow.'

After much thought he took off his red knitted garter from his leg and tied it round the stem of the ragwort under which the Leprechaun had hidden his crock of gold – so he said.

'You have a head on you,' said the Leprechaun admiringly. 'Is that all you'll be wanting of me?'

'Thank you kindly,' said Tom as politely as you please now he'd got his own way. 'God speed you.'

'That's as it may be," said the Leprechaun, 'but you're welcome to what you find," and he disappeared amongst the ragwort. One moment he was there, the next he was not.

Tom set off as fast as he could for home. He didn't wait to change his Sunday suit – after all when he was rich with the Leprechaun's gold, he could buy as many new clothes as he liked. He caught up a spade and hurried back to the twenty-acre field. The field faced the sunset and he was fairly dazzled with the light of it in his eyes. 'I've never seen it look so red,' thought Tom and he began to search for his red garter. That was soon done for every single ragwort in the field was tied round with a red garter the like of his own!

Tom stood and stared. 'And what will I be doing now?' he said indignantly. 'It's the whole field I'd have to dig. All twenty acres of it!'

Well, Tom knew that he'd never do that in a year. 'Bad luck to you wherever you are!' he shouted to the Leprechaun, but the little man, wherever he was, lay low and made no answer.

Away went Tom back to the farm, feeling very sorry for himself, his clothes in such rags that he couldn't for very shame show himself at the dance.

And although he looked for a Leprechaun many times, he never set eyes on one again, nor on a crock of gold.

His Augustness
The Prince Fire-Fade

A Story from
Japan

THIS is a story of the days when Japan was called the
Land of Reeds and the gods went to and fro upon
it. One of them called Heaven's-Sun-Height wooed
and married the Princess-Blossoming-Brightly-as-the-
Flowers-of-the-Trees.

They had two sons, the eldest of whom was Prince

Fire-Flash and the younger, the Prince Fire-Fade. Prince Fire-Flash had the luck of the sea and caught things broad of fin and narrow of fin; and Prince Fire-Fade had the luck of the hills and caught things rough of hair and soft of hair.

One day the younger said to the elder, 'Let us exchange our luck,' and to this Prince Fire-Flash agreed. Prince Fire-Fade fished all day in the sea but he caught not so much as a sprat and, moreover, he lost his brother's fish-hook.

Prince Fire-Flash hunted all day on the hills and shot not so much as a squirrel, but he brought home his brother's bow and arrows. When he met his brother, he said, 'The luck of the hills is its own luck and the luck of the sea is its own luck. Let us take our own again.'

Then the younger brother was afraid and said, 'Your fish-hook was not a good fish-hook; I caught not a single fish with it; moreover I lost it in the sea.'

'It was my fish-hook. Give me my fish-hook!' said Prince Fire-Flash. He said it over and over again until at last his younger brother took off his sword and melted part of it in the fire and made of it five hundred fish-hooks.

'I want my own fish-hook,' grumbled Prince Fire-Flash and he would not accept those his brother had made.

The Prince Fire-Fade wept and, as he wept, the Deity Salt-Possessor came out of the sea and asked him why he grieved.

The Prince replied, 'My elder brother lent me a fish-hook and I lost it. I have given him many fish-hooks in its place, but he will not accept them.'

'I will give you good counsel,' said the Deity Salt-Possessor. He made Prince Fire-Fade a little boat and set him in it and said, 'When I have pushed off the boat, go your way until you come to the sea-path. It is a pleasant path and at the end of it you will come to a palace of fishes' scales which belongs to the Great Deity Ocean-Possessor. Beside the gate there is a well and above the well there is a many-branching cassia-tree. Sit there and the Great Deity's daughter will see you and give you good counsel.'

So the Prince Fire-Fade went by the sea-path till he came to the palace of fishes' scales. Beside the gate there was a well, a clear-spring well at the bottom of the sea, and above the well there was a many-branching cassia-tree. As he sat in its branches, the maidens of the Sea-Deity's daughter came to draw water in their jewelled pails. They were much astonished to see the shining of the Prince Fire-Fade reflected in the water and, looking up, they saw him in the tree.

The Prince asked for a drink and they gave it to him in a jewelled goblet. When he had drunk, he took the magnificent jewel that hung round his neck and dropped it into the goblet and the maidens carried it to their mistress, the Sea-Deity's daughter, Princess Many-Jewels.

'Where did this jewel come from?' asked the Princess, and her maidens told her of the handsome young man in the cassia-tree.

The Princess Many-Jewels arose and went through

the gate and stood beside the well. She looked up and saw a young man and he looked down and saw a young maid and their glances met. The Princess went to her father and said, 'There is a handsome young man at our gate.'

The Great Deity Ocean-Possessor arose and went to look and recognized the august son of the god Heaven's-Sun-Height. He brought Prince Fire-Fade into the palace and spread upon the floor eight skins of sea-asses and eight rugs of silk. He made him a feast of all things rare in the sea and gave him the hand of the Princess Many-Jewels in marriage.

For three years Prince Fire-Fade dwelt at the bottom of the sea and forgot all else. At the end of three years, he remembered the fish-hook and, remembering, he heaved a great sigh. The Princess Many-Jewels heard it and went to her father.

'For three years Prince Fire-Fade has lived with us and never has he sighed,' she said. 'Last night he heaved a great sigh. What can ail him?'

Her father went to the young man and said, 'What is the meaning of this sigh and, now that I think of it, what was the meaning of your coming to us in the first place?'

Prince Fire-Fade told him of the fish-hook and how he had lost it and did not dare to return to his brother without it. Then the Great Deity Ocean-Possessor assembled before him all the fishes of the sea, great and small, and told them the story. 'Has any one of you taken this fish-hook?' he asked.

The fishes replied with one voice, 'Of late the red *tai* has complained of something in its throat, by reason of which it is unable to eat. Doubtless it is the fish-hook.'

Then the *tai* was brought, very weak and thin, and commanded to open its mouth and, lo! in its mouth was the fish-hook. They took the fish-hook out and washed it and presented it respectfully to Prince Fire-Fade. The *tai* was greatly pleased and promptly ate many of the fishes there present.

The Deity Ocean-Possessor summoned together all the crocodiles and said, 'The august child of the god Heaven's-Sun-Height is about to proceed to the Upper Land. Which of you will escort him?' The crocodiles made answer, one by one according to their length, until the crocodile one fathom long offered to escort the prince.

'Do so,' said the Deity Ocean-Possessor, 'but while crossing the middle of the sea, do not harm him.'

He set Prince Fire-Fade on the head of the crocodile and accompanied him a little way. Then the crocodile escorted the Prince to the shore, being careful not to alarm him, and when he took his leave Prince Fire-Fade presented his pocket-knife to the crocodile.

Prince Fire-Fade hastened to return the long-lost fish-hook to his brother and they made their peace and lived together.

One day as Prince Fire-Fade walked on the beach, he saw someone coming by way of the sea-path. It was the Princess Many-Jewels. Then he was full of joy and together they built a house at the edge of the waves and thatched it with cormorants' feathers.

There came a night when the Princess Many-Jewels said to Prince Fire-Fade, 'This is the night when I must return to my land, so leave me.'

The Prince left her as she desired but, feeling curious,

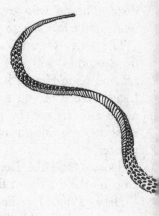

he returned at midnight and looked through the thatch. To his dismay he saw that there was a great dragon of the sea with his wife. The Prince was afraid and cried out.

Then the Princess came out and said sadly, 'I had wished to come and go across the sea-path always, but now I can never return to you.' So saying she gave their baby son into his father's arms and went out along the sea-path, the dragon with her, down to the depths of the sea.

The Prince took his son and cried to her to come back, but she would not hear. Only, in a little while, because she could not control her heart, she sent her younger sister, the Jewel-Good princess, to nurse the child.

But never again did Prince Fire-Fade see his wife, the beautiful Princess Many-Jewels.

The Woman of
the Sea

A Story from
Scotland

ONE clear summer night, a young man was walking
on the sand by the sea on the Isle of Unst. He had been
all day in the hayfields and was come down to the shore
to cool himself, for it was the full moon and the wind
blowing fresh off the water.

As he came to the shore he saw the sand shining white

in the moonlight and on it the sea-people dancing. He had never seen them before, for they show themselves like seals by day, but on this night, because it was mid-summer and a full moon, they were dancing for joy. Here and there he saw dark patches where they had flung down their sealskins, but they themselves were as clear as the moon itself, and they cast no shadow.

He crept a little nearer, and his own shadow moved before him, and of a sudden one of the sea-people danced upon it. The dance was broken. They looked about and saw him and with a cry they fled to their sealskins and dived into the waves. The air was full of their soft crying and splashing.

But one of the fairy-people ran hither and thither on the sands, wringing her hands as if she had lost something. The young man looked and saw a patch of darkness in his own shadow. It was a seal's skin. Quickly he threw it behind a rock and watched to see what the sea-fairy would do.

She ran down to the edge of the sea and stood with her feet in the foam, crying to her people to wait for her, but they had gone too far to hear. The moon shone on her and the young man thought she was the loveliest creature he had ever seen. Then she began to weep softly to herself and the sound of it was so pitiful that he could bear it no longer. He stood upright and went down to her.

'What have you lost, woman of the sea?' he asked her.

She turned at the sound of his voice and looked at him, terrified. For a moment he thought she was going to dive into the sea. Then she came a step nearer and held up her two hands to him.

'Sir,' she said, 'give it back to me and I and my people will give you the treasure of the sea.' Her voice was like the waves singing in a shell.

'I would rather have you than the treasure of the sea,' said the young man. Although she hid her face in her hands and fell again to crying, more hopeless than ever, he was not moved.

'It is my wife you shall be,' he said. 'Come with me now to the priest, and we will go home to our own house, and it is yourself shall be mistress of all I have. It is warm you will be in the long winter nights, sitting at your own hearth stone and the peat burning red, instead of swimming in the cold green sea.'

She tried to tell him of the bottom of the sea where there comes neither snow nor darkness of night and the waves are as warm as a river in summer, but he would not listen. Then he threw his cloak around her and lifted her in his arms and they were married in the priest's house.

He brought her home to his little thatched cottage and into the kitchen with its earthen floor, and set her down before the hearth in the red glow of the peat. She cried out when she saw the fire, for she thought it was a strange crimson jewel.

'Have you anything as bonny as that in the sea?' he asked her, kneeling down beside her and she said, so faintly that he could scarcely hear her, 'No.'

'I know not what there is in the sea,' he said, 'but

there is nothing on land as bonny as you.' For the first time she ceased her crying and sat looking into the heart of the fire. It was the first thing that made her forget, even for a moment, the sea which was her home.

All the days she was in the young man's house, she never lost the wonder of the fire and it was the first thing she brought her children to see. For she had three children in the twice seven years she lived with him. She was a good wife to him. She baked his bread and she spun the wool from the fleece of his Shetland sheep.

He never named the seal's skin to her, nor she to him, and he thought she was content, for he loved her dearly and she was happy with her children. Once, when he was ploughing on the headland above the bay, he looked down and saw her standing on the rocks and crying in a mournful voice to a great seal in the water. He said nothing when he came home, for he thought to himself it was not to wonder at if she were lonely for the sight of her own people. As for the seal's skin, he had hidden it well.

There came a September evening and she was busy in the house, and the children playing hide-and-seek in the stacks in the gloaming. She heard them shouting and went out to them.

'What have you found?' she said.

The children came running to her. 'It is like a big cat,' they said, 'but it is softer than a cat. Look!' She looked and saw her seal's skin that was hidden under last year's hay.

She gazed at it, and for a long time she stood still. It

was warm dusk and the air was yellow with the after-glow of the sunset. The children had run away again, and their voices among the stacks sounded like the voices of birds. The hens were on the roost already and now and then one of them clucked in its sleep. The air was full of little friendly noises from the sleepy talking of the swallows under the thatch. The door was open and the warm smell of the baking of bread came out to her.

She turned to go in, but a small breath of wind rustled over the stacks and she stopped again. It brought a sound that she had heard so long she never seemed to hear it at all. It was the sea whispering down on the sand. Far out on the rocks the great waves broke in a boom, and close in on the sand the little waves slipped racing back. She took up the seal's skin and went swiftly down the track that led to the sands. The children saw her and cried to her to wait for them, but she did not hear them. She was just out of sight when their father came in from the byre and they ran to tell him.

'Which road did she take?' said he.

'The low road to the sea,' they answered, but already their father was running to the shore. The children tried to follow him, but their voices died away behind him, so fast did he run.

As he ran across the hard sands, he saw her dive to join the big seal who was waiting for her, and he gave a loud cry to stop her. For a moment she rested on the surface of the sea, then she cried with her voice that was like the waves singing in a shell, 'Fare ye well, and all good befall you, for you were a good man to me.'

Then she dived to the fairy places that lie at the bottom of the sea and the big seal with her.

For a long time her husband watched for her to come back to him and the children; but she came no more.

The Fairy Rath

A Story from
Ireland

THERE was once a man who had the misfortune to be
a hunchback, but he was a kindly man and a happy
one. He was poor, although he worked hard, and everyone knew him to be an honest fellow.

One day as he climbed a steep hill in Ulster, he came to a great circular mound enclosing a broad sweep of grass which shone green in the light of the setting sun. It looked like a fort but there were no men-at-arms to be seen, for it was a rath, a dwelling place for fairies.

The hunchback was a little scared to be so near a place where fairies lived, but being very tired he sat down for a short rest, leaning his head against the mound of earth. As he rested there in the half-light, he heard a deep humming like the buzzing of a thousand bees from inside the mound.

He listened and soon he made out words in the humming and knew that he was hearing the singing of the fairies inside the mound. It was Irish they were singing, and this was their song, over and over again:

> Da Luan, Da Mart,
> Da Luan, Da Mart.

'Faith,' thought the hunchback, 'that's not much of a song. Da Luan, Da Mart – Monday, Tuesday – why not Wednesday as well?'

So he sang very softly to himself:

> Da Luan, Da Mart,
> Agus da Cadin!

because he liked the sound of it better with 'And Wednesday' added to it.

The humming inside the rath stopped as though the fairies were listening. When the hunchback had sung the new words often enough for them to get them by heart, they began singing themselves:

> Da Luan, Da Mart,
> Agus da Cadin!

It was such a happy sound that the little hunchback was pleased too.

The rath opened and out came the fairies, the Good People, smiling. They beckoned him to follow them into the hillside and there he saw a great hall lit by thousands of glow-worms. A feast was spread on long tables and soon the hunchback was eating good things the like of which he had never tasted before. At the end of the feast the chief of the fairies called him and bade him kneel before him. 'Friend, you have something you do not need!' he said and struck him lightly on his hump. When the little man stood up, he was as straight as any man in Ulster, for his hump had disappeared.

Happily the little man wandered about the great hall admiring its splendours. Great pieces of gold were scattered about the floor but the Good People walked carelessly over them as though they were worthless. There were gorse bushes growing in the hall too, for the Good People love their golden flowers.

'Would you like some fairy gold to remember us by?' asked the chief of the fairies.

'I would that,' said the little man.

'Then fill your pockets,' said the chief leading him to a gorse bush and pointing at the golden flowers.

The little man was astonished. What use were golden

flowers to him? He was poor and could have done with some of the gold pieces that lay everywhere, but he was too kind to say that he would prefer these to the flowers. He thanked the chief politely and filled his pockets with the gorse blossoms. 'Bless the Good People – they know no better!' he thought to himself, and he made as much of the golden flowers as if they had been golden sovereigns.

The fairies led the little man out of the rath and he heard them humming and singing their new song beneath him. To the sound of that music he fell asleep for he had no fear of the mound now – the Good People were his friends.

When he awoke in the clear morning light, the mound was green and quiet and there was no sign of the fairies. 'It must have been a dream,' thought the little man, but when he stood up he felt freer than ever before in his life, for his hump had gone and his back was really as straight as that of any man in Ulster. In

great delight he put his hands in his pockets, for they felt strangely heavy. Instead of yellow flowers, he found solid lumps of gold! He need never be poor again.

The story was told all over the country and everyone was glad for the little hunchback. But another man who was a hunchback heard the story, a mean man with a mind as crooked as his back. He saw no reason why he too should not be lucky and lose his hump and collect some gold into the bargain, so he hurried to the fairy rath and lay down with his ear against it.

Sure enough the fairies were singing with all their might:

Da Luan, Da Mart,
Agus da Cadin!

'Little fools!' said the hunchback to himself and he shouted at the top of his voice, 'What about Friday?'

Now Friday is a day the fairies never name to each other for, as everyone knows, it is an unlucky day. So when they heard the hunchback shouting at them in his coarse voice, they began to buzz like bees, but angry bees. Out of the rath they came and beckoned the hunchback in to join their feast. The man rubbed his hands with glee when he saw the tables covered with food. He pushed the Good People aside roughly, sat down at the table and began to eat greedily, snatching food by handfuls from the loaded dishes.

When he had done, the chief of the fairies bade him kneel. 'Not I,' said the hunchback. 'I kneel to no man.'

The chief said nothing, but struck the hunchback

smartly on his back and asked him whether he would like some fairy gold.

'I would that!' said the man.

The chief pointed to the gorse blossom. 'Fill your pockets,' he said.

'Is it filling my pockets with that rubbish I will be?' he said to himself. He stooped and pretended to be picking the flowers but, unseen as he thought, he stuffed as many gold pieces as he could into his pockets and even into the front of his coat.

The fairies made no sign that they had seen him do this. They did not challenge him, but gravely bade him goodnight and disappeared into the rath again. There was a sound like laughter within and then all was silent.

The hunchback fell asleep. When he awoke it was broad daylight. He put his hands into his pockets to feel his gold, but there was nothing in them but a few faded gorse blossoms. Not a single gold piece remained.

Well, at least he would have lost his hump, he thought, but his back seemed strangely heavy and when he looked at his reflection in a forest pool he saw that he now had two humps – his own and that of the kindly little hunchback whose good fortune he had coveted.

What happened to him afterwards, why, no man knows.

The Magic Horse

A Story from
Persia

ONCE upon a time there was a great King in Persia.
He made a feast and, as he sat on his throne with his
three daughters and son beside him, three wise men
came and bowed before him. One brought a peacock of

gold, the second a trumpet of brass, the third a horse
of ebony and ivory.

'What are these?' asked the King.

'O King of the Age,' said the first wise man. 'At the
end of every hour the peacock will flap its golden wings
and scream: so shall you know the passing of the
hours.'

'O King,' said the second wise man. 'Set the trumpet
at the gate of the city, and if a man that is your enemy
pass through it, the trumpet will blow: so shall your
enemy be known and taken.'

'O King,' said the third wise man. 'If a man ride
upon this horse, it will carry him to whatever country
he pleases.'

Then said the King, 'I will give no gifts till I have
proved these marvels.' He tried the peacock and it
screamed at each hour, and the trumpet and it blew
when his enemy approached.

'Ask what you will,' said the King to the two wise
men.

'Marry us to thy two daughters,' said the wise men,
and it was done. Then the third wise man came forward
and bowed to the ground and said, 'O King of the Age,
do to me as you have done to them."

'Not until I have tried the horse,' said the King.

'O my father,' said the Prince, the King's son, 'let me
ride the horse.'

So the Prince mounted the horse, and struck his spurs
into it, but it did not move.

'How now,' said he to the wise man and the man

came forward bowing, and showed him a little screw. 'Turn it, O Prince,' he said.

The Prince turned the screw and up shot the horse into the air till it was hidden in the clouds, and all the people stood gaping. Then the King scattered dust on his head and lamented, for he thought that his son had been carried off by an evil spirit. At once he threw the wise man into prison.

Now when the Prince found himself flying through the air, he was afraid. He looked at the horse and saw that on its right shoulder it had something like the head of a cock and the same on the left. He turned the screw on the right shoulder and the horse flew upwards even more swiftly; he turned the screw on the left and it began to go downwards very gently. Then the Prince was glad and took pleasure in his horse. He began to descend to the earth, for he was a great way off.

As he flew, he looked at the countries and cities beneath him, but none of them did he know. Towards the end of the day he passed above a city splendid and fair, set in the midst of rivers and trees. It was drawing towards sunset and he thought to himself, 'It is the fairest city I have seen. I will spend the night there – tomorrow I will go home to my father and tell him all that I have seen.'

Very slowly he passed above the city, looking for a place where he might come down without being seen. In the midst of the city he saw a palace, flat-roofed, and around it a great garden wall. 'This is a good place,' he said and turned the screw to go down.

The horse floated down like a bird till it stood on the palace roof and the Prince dismounted. 'By Allah!' he said, 'he who made you was a great magician. When I return home I will seek him out and show him much favour.'

The Prince sat on the palace roof, waiting till the darkness fell. One by one the stars came out in the sky and lights shone out in the houses below him. There was a pleasant smell of cooking in the warm air which roused the Prince's hunger, but he did not dare go down from the roof until every one should be asleep.

As soon as the palace seemed quiet and dark, the Prince went down a flight of steps which led to a marble court where a fountain played and the air was scented with myrtle. All the rooms in the palace opened from it, but there was no light in any of them and no one stirred. There was no sound but the falling of the water and no breath of any living thing. Perplexed, he thought to himself, 'I will go and spend the night beside my horse, and when it is daybreak I will mount and away, for I do not like the strangeness of this place.'

Even as he thought this, he saw a light shining down the corridor. He hid behind a clump of myrtles to watch. The light came nearer and he saw a company of slave girls, walking by torchlight, and among them a damsel as slender as the branch of the willow and radiant as the full moon. She was the daughter of the King of the city which was Sana in Arabia, and her father loved her so greatly that he had caused this palace to be built for her.

Whenever she was weary she came here with her maids for a day or two.

This evening she was restless and had come by night with her maids and a guard walking behind her with his sword drawn. They passed down the corridors and scattered through the palace so that it sprang into life with lights and laughter. They spread cushions in the Princess's room and sprinkled perfume and threw flowers at one another: jasmine of Aleppo and water-lilies of Damascus, anemones and violets; and the darkness of the courtyard was like a wall beyond them.

Even as they laughed, the Prince sprang in upon them from the blue night, rushed at the guard, struck him to the ground and caught up his sword. The slave girls scattered to this side and that, so that there was no one between him and the Princess. He stood gazing at her, with the light sparkling on the sword and the jewels on his turban, and the Princess sat amid her silken cushions and looked at him without fear. At last she spoke.

'Are you,' she said, 'the king's son who asked me in marriage of my father yesterday, and my father refused him, for that he said he was very hideous? By Allah, my father lied, for you are a handsome young man.'

She took his hand and seated him beside her. The slave girls ran to the guard where he lay upon the ground. 'Behold!' they said, 'the young man who threw you on the ground is sitting with the King's daughter.'

The guard arose shaking. He drew the curtain and saw the Princess and the Prince sitting talking together, and he cried out, 'O my master, are you a man or a

Jinn?' for he feared the stranger who had come out of the night.

Then the Prince arose in wrath. 'Dost thou take the son of the Persian Kings for a son of unbelieving devils? Woe to you, O most evil of slaves!'

Then the guard went from the palace and knelt before the King of that country. 'O King,' he cried, 'a devil of the Jinn in the form of the son of the Persian Kings has taken your daughter.'

The King hastened to the palace and found the slave girls standing idle in the ante-room. 'O King,' they cried, 'as we sat with the Princess, there rushed upon us this young man shining like the full moon with a drawn sword in his hand, and we do not know whether he be man or Jinn.'

Then the King went forward and looked through the curtain and there sat the Prince on the divan and the Princess beside him, talking.

Then rage grew upon the King and he pulled aside the curtain and rushed upon the Prince. The young man shouted at the King with an amazing shout which terrified him, and came at him with his sword. The King saw that he was stronger than himself and he sheathed his sword and met him with politeness.

'If you are indeed the son of the Persian Kings, how is it that you came to my daughter by stealth? Know that I have slain kings and the sons of kings for naming her name to me.'

Then said the Prince, 'Let us fight for her, I and thou, or bring me against thy whole army and I will fight against them. If I overcome them, then am I fit to be son-in-law to the King.'

At daybreak the King sent for his men-at-arms, a thousand thousand. 'Know,' he said, 'that a young man has come to me to ask my daughter in marriage. Never have I seen a handsomer than he, nor one stronger in heart; for he says that he alone will do battle with you, and overcome you. So receive him upon the point of your spears, for he has undertaken a great enterprise.'

Then the Prince was brought out. But he said, 'O King, how shall a man that is on foot fight with men mounted on horses?'

'Here is my own horse,' said the King.

'I will not fight except on my own horse,' said the Prince. 'Command it to be brought from the roof of the palace.'

'He is mad,' said the King. 'How shall a horse be on the roof?' But when he sent slaves to look, they brought back the ebony horse and all marvelled at its beauty.

Then said the Prince, 'Bid the troops go back a bow-shot that I may charge them.' And when the ground was clear he mounted the horse and turned the pin and the horse rose up into the sky.

'Take him,' cried the King. 'Take him before he escapes!' But the captains made answer that they could not catch a flying bird or an enchanter.

Then the King went back to the palace and came to his daughter. 'O my daughter,' he said, 'praise Allah for our escape from this crafty enchanter.' But when the Princess heard that the Prince had gone from them like a bird into the air, she turned away her face and prayed to be taken to her own palace. There she sat and wept and would not be comforted.

The Prince journeyed till he came in sight of the city of his father in Persia and came down in the palace yard. His father made great joy of him for he had thought he was dead. He brought the wise man out of prison and put rich robes on him and gave him presents. But the King did not give the wise man the youngest princess to wife, because he was so hideous. This made the wise man angry and he repented that he had given the magic horse to the King and plotted to steal it back again.

That night there was a feast in the palace and a slave took a lute and began to sing love songs. Then the Prince remembered the Princess in the city of Sana. He waited until all were asleep, mounted his horse, turned the pin and flew up under the stars. All night he travelled, finding his way by the moon, and at dawn he came to the city of Sana and the roof of the palace, and there he descended.

He went down the stairway to the room where he had seen the Princess, but she was not there. He went through the palace seeking her, and at last he found her lying, weeping for sorrow.

'O my Princess,' he said, 'why art thou weeping?'

'I thought thou wouldst never return,' she said.

'O my Princess,' said the Prince, 'wilt thou come with me to my country?'

'With all my heart,' she said.

The Prince was glad and he took her hand and led her swiftly through the sleeping palace and up the stairs to the roof. There he set her behind him on the horse and fastened her to him with his girdle and the horse swept up into the air. But at that moment the slave girls came running and her father heard and saw the horse already high in the air. He cried to the Prince, 'Have mercy upon me and her mother, for our daughter is very dear to us!'

The Prince heard and spoke to the Princess. 'O Desire of the Age,' he asked, 'is it your will to go back?'

'O my Master,' she answered, 'it is my will to be with you wherever you go.'

Then the Prince was glad and made the horse go softly lest she should be frightened. At noon they halted in a green meadow where there was a spring of water and at sunset they drew near his father's city.

Now the Prince wished to bring the Princess into the city with all ceremony, for she was a Princess of Arabia. Beyond the city walls was a private garden where the King sometimes came at evening. There were pools covered with lilies and a summer pavilion. Here he came down and brought her into the pavilion to rest.

'Wait here,' he said, 'till I send my messenger,' and he departed, leaving the magic horse at the door.

The keepers of the garden were talking as he went out on foot and took no note of him. So he came to the palace, and his father was glad when he saw him and heard of the coming of the Princess.

All the city was hung with lanterns and silken hangings. The King went out to meet the Princess with his guards and noblemen in great magnificence. Before him rode the Prince and there was a litter of scarlet and gold and green brocade for the Princess. When the Prince came near the garden, he dismounted and went on alone to find the Princess. It was dewfall and the garden was dim as he hurried to the pavilion where he had left her.

The pavilion was empty and the horse was gone. 'Did any one enter the garden this evening?' the Prince asked the gardeners, but they said they had seen no one except the wise man come to gather herbs. Then the Prince rent his clothes for he knew at once that it was the wise man who had taken away the Princess.

What had happened was this: the wise man had gone to gather herbs and, as he stopped to pick them, he smelt the fragrance of jasmine and followed it to find where it grew. So he came to the summer pavilion and, looking through the trellis, saw the Princess and the ebony horse.

The wise man went in to the Princess and kissed the ground before her, but when the Princess saw how hideous he was, she was frightened.

'Who are you?' she asked.

'O my mistress, the Prince sent me to bring you nearer the city where he awaits you,' answered the wise man. 'He is with the King his father and comes to meet you in state.'

But the Princess was still afraid. 'Could he find no one to send but you?' she said.

The wise man laughed and said, 'Verily, he chose me because I am ugly and old.'

'What shall I ride on?' asked the Princess.

'The horse on which you came.'

'I cannot ride it by myself,' said the Princess.

'Then I will ride with you,' said the wise man, smiling. He took her behind him on the horse, and bound her to him and turned the pin, and the horse shot up into the sky, travelling so swiftly that the city was left far behind.

'This is not what my lord told you to do!' cried the Princess. 'Woe to you!'

'The horse was mine,' said the wise man, 'and he took it. This night I have found both it and you, and shall torture his heart as he has tortured mine.'

Then the Princess fell to weeping, crying, 'I have left my father and mother, and now my lover is taken from me.'

'I care not for that,' said the wise man and carried her further and further away.

As for the Prince, he set out on foot to find the Princess and her captor. He sought them from city to city, but he heard no news of them, for to fly by air leaves no trace. For many moons he travelled and late one night he came to an inn. A party of merchants had ar-arrived before him and sat talking, and one said: 'By Allah, I heard of a strange thing that befell the King of the Greeks. He went out to hunt and his court with him. In a green meadow by the river he saw a man of hideous countenance, and a young girl whose like he had never seen for beauty, and an ebony horse. The old man said the girl was his wife, but the young girl protested that she was not and that he had taken her by force and craftiness.'

'And what befell them?' asked the other merchants, while the Prince strained to hear.

'The King commanded the old man to be thrown into prison, but the young girl he took home with him to the palace. What became of the ebony horse, I do not know.'

'Sir,' said the Prince, 'do you know the name of the King and the city?' The merchant told him. That night the Prince slept well, for he knew he was near the end of his quest.

He was up and on the road at dawn, but with all the speed he could make, it was sunset when he came to the city. The King of that city delighted to see all strangers, but as it was late, the Prince was taken for safe keeping to the prison.

'By Allah,' said the keepers of the prison, 'he is a comely young man. He shall eat out of our own dish.' So the Prince sat down with them outside the prison and shared their meal, and when it was over, they sat and talked.

'O young man,' said one, 'from what country do you come?'

'From Persia,' answered the Prince.

'There is a second Persian in the prison,' said the gaoler laughing. 'Never have I seen a greater liar than he. He pretends that he is a wise man. The King found him and a young woman with him and an ebony horse.'

'And what became of the woman?' asked the Prince.

'As for the woman, she is in the King's palace and he

loves her, but she is mad. If the Persian were a wise man, as he pretends, he would cure her, for the King is for ever seeking a remedy for her madness.'

'And what of the horse?'

'The horse is in the King's treasury,' said the keeper of the prison.

When morning came the Prince was brought before the King of the city.

'What is thy country,' said the King, 'and what is thy trade?'

'O King,' said the young man, 'I am of Persia and I am a man of science : I cure the sick and the mad. I go from city to city seeking wisdom.'

'O excellent sage,' said the King, 'in a good hour art thou come.' He told the Prince of the madness of the Princess and how he had found her.

'O King,' said the young man, 'what have you done with the horse? It may have to do with her madness.' For he thought to himself, 'If the horse is safe, I shall escape with the Princess, but if the horse is broken, I must find some other way to rescue her.'

The King led him to the treasury where the horse stood and it was safe and sound. 'Now, bring me to the damsel,' said the Prince. 'It may be that I can cure her by means of this horse.'

Now the Princess was not really mad, but only pretending it so that the King would not marry her. When the Prince came to her, he found her beating herself and feigning madness.

'O Desire of the Age,' he said, and when she heard his

voice, the Princess gave a great cry and swooned. The Prince knelt beside her till she came to herself and he whispered in her ear what she must do. She lay quiet and he went out to the King and told him that he had freed her from the spirit of madness that was tormenting her.

The King was glad, for he loved her. He went in to see her and she spoke to him graciously. He sent for slaves to wait on her and they put royal robes on her and jewels on her neck.

'O excellent sage,' said the King, 'the blessing of Allah be upon thee! Ask what thou wilt, for the cure is wonderful.'

'O King,' said the young man, 'the cure is not yet ended, for I must bind fast the evil spirit that tormented her, so that he may never come back. Come with your guards to the meadow where thou didst find her at the first, and bring the damsel and the ebony horse with thee, so that the thing may be done.'

A great company followed the King to the green meadow by the river.

'Command the troops to stand a great way off,' said the Prince, 'and set the damsel and the ebony horse by themselves, for I must burn incense round them and so imprison the evil spirit.'

So was it done. The Prince scattered incense in a ring and as the smoke of it spread in a cloud, he took the Princess behind him on the horse and rose into the sky.

'Truly the man is a great enchanter!' said the King. For half a day he and all his court stood gazing upwards, waiting for the damsel and the youth to return. When they did not, he returned to the city and his wrath was great. After a time he allowed the wise man to go free from the prison, but none heard of him again.

As for the Prince and the Princess, they journeyed to Persia. For a month there was feasting and rejoicing and, at the end of it, they were married. The King sent rich presents to the father and mother of the Princess and they were content with what had befallen her.

But on the night of the Prince's marriage, his father broke the magic horse into a thousand pieces, for in his wisdom he deemed it to be evil rather than good.

The Queen
Taken by Faerie

A Story from
Scotland

THE great King, Orfeo, was a mighty hunter and cour-
teous, and above all things he loved the sound of the
harp. All the great harpers in the world passed at some
time through his city and he did them honour; but he
himself was the greatest harper of them all. Men stood

dreaming when he played, for it seemed to them that they were in heaven.

Orfeo's queen, the Lady Heurodis, was the fairest lady that ever was. So full of delight was she that no man had words to describe her. Her husband loved her beyond all else.

It came about one morning in May, when the days were mild and the hail-showers gone and every bough breaking into flower, that the Queen with two of her maidens went to the apple-orchard to hear the birds sing. They sat, all three, under a fair blossoming tree and, in a little while, the Queen fell asleep on the grass. Long she slept, until the late afternoon.

When she awoke it was with a great cry. She tore her rich robes like one that had lost her wits, and wept bitterly. Her two maids ran to the palace in terror, crying that their Queen had gone mad. Quickly her ladies came and carried her to her bed and there they held her, for she cried out constantly and strove to escape.

Then came the King and watched her in great pity. 'Dear life,' he said, 'what ails thee? Tell me what it is that I may help thee.'

The Queen lay still at last and began to weep softly. 'Alas, my lord,' she said, 'never once was there anger between us since we were wed. I have loved thee as my life and thou me. But now we must part.'

'That shall never be!' cried the King.

'Hear what befell me while I slept,' said the Queen. 'As I lay in the orchard asleep, there came to me knights in armour and bade me come and speak with their lord

the king. I answered their bold words that I could not come, and they rode away. Then came their king with a hundred knights and damsels riding on snow-white horses and clad in white: I never saw any so fair. The king had a crown on his head of one precious stone which shone as bright as the sun. He made me ride on a palfrey beside him, whether I would or no, and brought me to his palace. Castles and towers he showed me, rivers and forests and flowering fields, and then he brought me home again.

' "Lady," he said, "look to it that you wait here for me tomorrow under this same apple tree, for you shall live in my land for ever." '

Then Orfeo cried that he would rather lose his life than his lady. When it came to the hour of noon on the next day, he went with the Queen to the apple tree and with him a company of knights in armour. They surrounded their Queen and swore that they would die, every man of them, before they would allow her to be taken away.

Then, before their very eyes the Queen went from them; and none saw her go. One moment she was there, the next she was not. Sadly the King returned to the palace and none dared speak to him.

At long last the King came and called his knights to him. 'My lords,' he said, 'before you here I ordain my High Steward to be over my kingdom in my stead. Without my Queen, I cannot live. I go to the wilderness and there will I stay to the end, among the wild things of the wood. When you hear of my death, choose you a new king. Do your best with all that which was mine.'

At the King's words, all that were in the hall prayed him not to go from them, but he said, 'So shall it be.' He took his harp and went barefoot through the gate. Through the wood and over the heath he went to the wilderness.

He that had worn silk lay now on the heather and covered himself with leaves; he that once had castles and towers, wandered the woods in frost and snow; he to whom knights and ladies had knelt, had now no friends.

In summer he lived on berries and wild fruit, in winter on nuts and roots. His harp he hid in a hollow tree, but when there was shining weather he took it out and played it. At the sound of his harping, the wild things that lived in the wood came and stood round him to hear and the birds on the briars were still. Ten years passed thus and his beard grew down to his girdle and his face was thin and sad.

Sometimes the King of Faerie swept past him with his hunt, with the blowing of horns and the baying of hounds: but what prey they hunted he knew not, nor whither it was they vanished. Sometimes he saw a great host, a thousand knights in battle array, with lances and banners, but to what battle they rode he never knew. Often he saw knights and ladies come dancing, quaintly clad and quaintly pacing, but what it was they danced he did not know.

There came a day when he saw a company of ladies riding. Gentle and gay they were and no man rode amongst them. Each lady had a falcon on her wrist, for they were hawking by the river where the mallard and the heron and the wild goose haunted. The King watched and laughed: 'By my faith,' he said, 'it is long since I saw the like. I will go nearer.'

Even as he came out of the wood, one of the ladies turned and looked upon him, and he knew her for his own Queen. When she saw how lean and worn he was, the tears fell from her eyes. Then the ladies swept her away.

When he came out of his trance, he flung his harp

upon his shoulder and followed after, stumbling and falling and rising again. On rode the ladies till they came to a rock. Into the cleft of the rock they rode and the King followed after, and of a sudden he came out into a fair green land, shining like a summer's day.

In the midst of the land stood a castle, clear as crystal. Crystal were the walls and the buttresses arched with red gold: within were broad ways paved with precious stones. There was no night in the land for, when the sun set, the stones of the palace glimmered and at midnight they shone like high noon.

Into the castle the ladies rode. When Orfeo came up, the gates were shut so that he had to knock. The porter came and eyed him. 'What do you here?' he said.

Orfeo replied, 'I am a minstrel. I would play before the King.'

The porter let him in and led him through the castle. Within, Orfeo saw many that had been stolen away by the faerie folk. For the most part they lay asleep and among them he saw his own dear wife, Heurodis, sleeping under an apple tree, even as she had been taken.

The King of Faerie sat at table with his Queen beside him. When Orfeo was able to look upon their brightness, he kneeled before the King.

'Sire,' he said, 'if it please you, I would play to you.'

The King looked at him, kneeling there; and said, 'What man is this that has come hither? Never since I was King of Faerie was there a man so foolhardy as to come willingly to us.'

'Lord,' said Orfeo, 'I am but a poor minstrel and it

is the custom of such to seek the houses of great lords. Welcome or not, we must offer our skill.' And Orfeo began to play.

From far and near in the Faerie court they came to the sound of his playing, crowding softly through the doorways. On her throne the Queen sat still: so still that the shimmering lights of her crown trembled into one flame. The King's soul was drawn by Orfeo's harping as the sea is drawn by the moon. The music ceased and there was silence.

'Minstrel,' said the King, 'ask what you will and you shall have it.'

'Sire,' said Orfeo, 'I would have the lady who sleepeth yonder under the apple tree.'

The King looked where the fair Heurodis lay and from her to the strange gaunt man at his feet and forgot his promise. 'Nay,' he said, 'that shall never be. A sorry couple you would make, you that are so lean and grim and she that is so fair.'

'King,' said Orfeo, 'but one thing were more sorry, that the King should have forgotten his promise.'

'Take her by the hand and go,' said the King. 'I wish you joy of her.'

Then Orfeo gave him thanks. He took his wife by the hand and led her swiftly out of Faerie. By the way that he came, by that way he went and brought her to their own city. That night they lodged in a peasant's hut outside the gate, for the King was still disguised as a poor minstrel. He asked of the peasant how the kingdom fared and the man told him how ten years ago, the

Queen was stolen away by Faerie, and how the King went away into exile, no man knew where, and how the High Steward held the kingdom for him.

When morning came, the King left his wife with the peasant and went into the city. It was noon and the streets were full of men who stopped to gaze at him.

'Saw ye ever such a man,' they cried. 'Lo! his beard hangeth to his knees as ivy clingeth about an oak.' But the King went on with his harp on his shoulder till he met the High Steward face to face.

'Sir Steward,' he cried. 'Mercy! I am a poor harper. Help me in my distress.'

The Steward looked kindly upon him. 'Come with me,' said he. 'Thou shalt share with me this day, for every good harper is welcome to me for the love of my lord, the King.'

The High Steward sat at meat in his castle and many a baron with him. Trumpeters and taborers and harpers made melody; and there sat Orfeo quiet and still and watched and listened. When they ceased and there was quiet, he took his harp and tuned it and himself began to play. Never man heard harping so sweet. The Steward leaned from his seat and looked upon the harp and knew it for the King's

'Man,' he cried, 'where had you that harp?'

'Lord,' said the King, 'it was in a desert place. There in a hollow I found a man that the wild beasts had slain. The harp lay by him.'

'Woe is me!' cried the Steward. 'That was my lord

the King. Alas! What shall I do, that have lost so good a lord?'

Now King Orfeo knew that his steward was a true man. He stood up and said: 'Steward, what if I were Orfeo the King?'

Then all that were in the hall knew that it was indeed the King. They shouted with one voice: 'You are our lord and our King!' They took him to his room and bathed him and shaved his beard and robed him as a king, and went out in great procession to bring home the Queen. Great was the rejoicing!

So was Orfeo new crowned with his Queen the Lady Heurodis. Long they reigned and happily.

Some other Puffins you might enjoy

Hobberdy Dick

K. M. Briggs

Long ago, there was plenty of secret folk life in England, particularly hobgoblins who guarded the houses and lands and watched over the families who lived in them until their task was done and they were released.

Hobberdy Dick of Widford Manor in the Cotswolds, was a good and careful guardian but the new family who came in after the Civil War did not win his affection like the Culvers, whom he had known and liked for two hundred years. The Puritan city merchant and his spoilt wife worked their servants hard and forbade all country pleasures. There was no mumming or Maying, or Christmas dancing or Easter egg rolling now, and none of the comfortable fireside chats that Dick had loved in the past.

K. M. Briggs is a well-known authority on folk lore, and Hobberdy Dick is so memorable and charming a character that this book is very well worth reading, not just for its wealth of magic and historical material but for its fascinating story.

The Minnipins

Carol Kendall

Every good Minnipin should act exactly like the others, and have the same healthy respect for the leading family, the Periods. But Muggles, she was beginning to question the smug authority of the Periods and to sympathize more with Gummy the poet, Curley Green the painter, and Walter the Earl, the old antiquarian. So, when the eccentrics were outlawed from the village, Muggles went with them to build a new settlement high on a mountain, and for the first time in their lives they were all happy.

Then the old enemies of the Minnipin people found their way back into the Minnipin valley, but could the exiles ever make all the people in the village believe in their danger?

The Minnipins is one of those great and wise fantasies that enrich the imagination and also help us to see our own world more clearly.

A Wizard of Earthsea
Ursula Le Guin

The island of Gont, a single mountain that lifts its peak a mile above the storm-racked North-east Sea, is a land famous for wizards, and not the least famous of these was a boy called Sparrowhawk who first discovered his magic power when he defended his village against an enemy horde.

Later he was taken to Roke Island, home of the famous School for Wizards, where he grew daily in knowledge and skill, till pride tempted him to try certain dangerous powers before he was equipped to deal with them, and he let loose an evil shadow-beast in his land.

Every so often a fantasy is written which stands out from the multitude in its wisdom, its originality, and its unforgettable situations: this is such a book. It won the Hornbook Prize in 1969.

For readers of eleven and over.

Fattypuffs and Thinifers
Andre Maurois

Edmund Double loved food and was plump, like his mother, while Terry his brother could hardly wait to leave the table and was consequently very thin, like his father. Nonetheless, they were all very fond of each other and the boys were amazed when, happening by chance to take a moving staircase to the Country Under the Earth, they found themselves split up and thrust head-long into the midst of the dispute between the warring nations of the Fattypuffs and the Thinifers.

The sparkle and easy humour of Andre Maurois' book is certain to fascinate children of all ages as long as Fattypuffs and Thinifers co-exist and remain mutually indispensable.

Bottersnikes and Gumbles
S. A. Wakefield

Deep in the Australian bush, where the Spiny Anteater and the Kookaburra live, there are some even more unusual animals – Bottersnikes and Gumbles. Bottersnikes are ugly. They have green faces with slanting eyes, noses like cheesegraters, mean little mouths, and ears that turn red when they are angry, which is often.

Gumbles are little creatures who love to paddle in ponds (they can't actually swim) and are hopeless when they go all giggly.

When some Bottersnikes caught some nice round little Gumbles they discovered they could squeeze them to any shape they liked without hurting them, and that if they were pressed very hard they flattened out like pancakes and couldn't get back to their proper shapes without help.

'Useful,' growled the Bottersnike King. 'We can pop 'em into jam tins and squash 'em down hard so's they can't get away, and when I want some work done they'll be ready and waiting to do it.' And so began the long, comic struggle between the Gumbles and the Bottersnikes, for the Gumbles were much too clever to stay stuck in those pesky jam tins for long.

For readers of eight and over.

Once on a Time
A. A. Milne

A hilarious, topsy-turvy, and utterly magical tale of the famous wars between Euralia and Barodia, of the machinations of that fascinating but ambitious woman Countess Belvane, of magic swords, cloaks of darkness, a Prince turned into an animal, true love, a bad fairy, a good wish and a bad one, a magic ring, a reluctant king and a kingly lover, all topped off with a properly happy ending.

A. A. Milne always thought this book was his best one and it is easy to see why.

A Book of Princesses
selected by Sally Patrick Johnson

There is a time to read stories about people like yourself, and a time to read about people who are different. That is when you should read about princesses, for whether they are bullied or cherished, proud or simple, hardworking or spoilt, beautiful or long-nosed, they are always special.

In this book you will find every type of princess imaginable, some are nice, some are horrid, some pretty, some plain, and the stories about them have been told by such writers as Walter de la Mare, Oscar Wilde, Hans Andersen, Charles Dickens and George MacDonald.

The Giant under the Snow
John Gordon

A grassy mound like a gigantic hand with trees growing between the fingers, the crack of an invisible whip in the dark forest, a huge menacing dog following a bus-load of school children back to the city – or was it, as Mr Roberts claimed, merely a reflection in the window? Who are the faceless, leathery men, thin-legged and quick as spiders? What do they want from the three children, Jonk, Bill and Arf?

This is a fascinating, chilling story by a new writer. Not a book for the nervous, not a book to pick up at night for it cannot be put down until the terrifying climax is reached, when the giant stirs under the snow, and wakes!